The Worth
of a Ruby

The Worth
of a Ruby

LYA BADGLEY

atmosphere press

Published by Atmosphere Press

Cover design by Felipe Betim

Atmospherepress.com

*"No one has found the worth of the ruby of the heart;
its value cannot be estimated."*

- Sri Guru Granth Sahib

CHAPTER ONE – 1995

Mallory Jones

No turning back now. Seattle was finished – a closed door seven thousand miles away.

The plane landed at Rangoon's Mingladon International Airport after a series of ominous bumps on the rough runway. Mallory stalled at the top of the stairs, unable to breathe in the scorching heat. Behind her, another passenger cleared his throat with a hurry-up sound, so she started down. As she crossed the simmering tarmac, languid youths in green army uniforms cradled guns as they lounged in the shade. Reading about a country ruled by a military dictatorship was one thing – seeing armed soldiers everywhere was still a surprise. One of the young men returned her curious look with a bright smile. Mallory dipped her head in acknowledgment. She remembered being a teenager holding a weapon.

Perspiration snaked down her back in the sultry arrivals hall. The immigration line was short, but each traveler's passport was reviewed with excruciating deliberation. The excitement of arrival after the twenty-nine-hour journey dissolved into annoyance at the delay. She hated small people abusing their little bit of power. An officer gestured for her to approach. Perhaps feeling her enmity, he stamped her passport with a quick thud, wafting the odor of his garlic-infused lunch.

An astonished customs agent stared in disbelief at the assortment of expensive knives in Mallory's suitcase. "But I'm a chef," she explained to a trio of worried-looking officials. "See? I have a business visa."

After an hour of waiting for approval from an unseen higher-up allowing Mallory to keep her knives, she finally stepped out into a mad scrum of taxi drivers and porters, all pushing and shouting for her attention. The hammer of humidity and aggressive touts backed her up against the building. Her deliberately built tower of expectations crashed onto the steaming hot pavement. The golden ticket of a job opportunity didn't seem quite so marvelous now.

A whiff of mothballs and a tap on her shoulder. An ancient man stood before her wearing a faded black jacket and broken spectacles held together with tape. "May I be of assistance?" He extended his gnarled hand in a handshake. "My name is U Hlaing. I am heading into town, and we might share a taxi?"

"No, thank you." Mallory whipped out her automatic reply. A lifetime of well-meaning strangers had taught her to always, always, just say no.

His wrinkled smile sagged. "Of course," he said. "At least take this?" He handed her a crisp, ironed handkerchief.

She blotted her face – another whiff of mothballs. Something about the smell of camphor reminded her of childhood, but long ago before it became a time of dread. The man peered at her with worry and a hint of something else – a kind of *caring*. Like a tropical Santa Claus with gifts of kindness in his back pocket. Did the longyi everyone wore here even have pockets? She smiled.

"Thank you. Does the offer to share a ride still stand?"

"Of course!" U Hlaing clapped his hands at two boys squatting on the curb, and within seconds, she found herself seated in the back of a decrepit Toyota sedan chugging toward Rangoon, her bags stuffed into the trunk and a plastic bottle of cold water in her hand. Patches of pavement rushed by through rusted-out holes in the car's floor as her hair whipped around her face with little stinging kisses, but she didn't care.

Black-trunked trees with vivid scarlet blossoms lined the road. Wooden huts sold woven baskets, straw brooms, and terracotta cisterns large enough to hold a person. Everything appeared dusted with the same reddish earth. She inhaled the curious fragrance unique to Southeast Asia of sweet jasmine and sour sewage. Dense traffic clogged the route as they neared the city's center. An overloaded bus with people hanging on the back bumper belched a puffy cloud of black exhaust she tasted on her lips.

"Where are you staying?" U Hlaing had declined to sit next to her in the back, explaining it seemlier for him to be in front.

"I don't have a place yet." She pulled out her *Lonely Planet* guide with the names of the hotels she'd highlighted. "Are you familiar with these?"

He peered myopically through his thick eyeglasses. "I'm sorry, but I don't know. The addresses are downtown, near the river. Not the best place for a young lady alone. May I suggest the hotel where my granddaughter works? Many foreign visitors stay there."

***

The Bagan Inn on Po Sein Road was a two-story wood and stucco building surrounded by lofty trees and a well-tended garden. Spiky dark red and orange anthurium plants lined the driveway. As the taxi passed, a bare-chested man in shorts and a peaked straw hat paused his weeding of the vivid green lawn to smile and wave. Purple oleander flowers planted around the doorway of an adjacent building gave a sweet fragrance to the air at the end of the long drive. Mallory relaxed for the first time in weeks.

U Hlaing jumped out and hobbled into reception. He

returned, followed by a lovely woman in her late twenties with a frangipani blossom tucked into her glossy, upswept black hair. She had a curious yellow paste on each cheek in a stylized sunflower design.

"My granddaughter, Cho Cho," U Hlaing introduced. "She will take care of all your needs. Her English is excellent."

Mallory nodded hello. "My name is Mallory Jones. I want a room, please." She didn't ask how much a night in the lovely hotel might cost, delighted at the thought of having an expense account for the first time in her life.

After check-in and saying goodbye to U Hlaing, Mallory followed Cho Cho through an open common area to a modest but charming room. A window high in the wall framed tree branches; a teakwood armoire with built-in drawers held additional storage. Best of all, a glorious air conditioner hummed against the heat. She stretched her hands up into the beautifully-cool air.

"Please take a moment to freshen up." Cho Cho placed Mallory's bag on the bed. "A cold drink and light snack will wait for you in the room outside when you're ready. We can discuss what you want to do while visiting our country. I'll be happy to make any arrangements for you."

"Thank you." Mallory hesitated a moment and then asked, "May I ask you something?"

"Of course."

"What's on your face? Is it medicinal?"

Cho Cho touched her cheek and smiled. "This is thanaka. Most Burmese women put it on in the morning. It is cooling for the skin with a sweet fragrance, like sandalwood. Now, may I ask *you* a question, Miss Mallory?"

"Sure." Mallory liked the young woman's spirit, peeking out from behind the polite veneer.

"Why have you come to Burma?"

Long answer or short? Mallory opted for the simplest reply. "I'm here to open a restaurant."

CHAPTER TWO

Thierry Aubert

Paris shone in the fleeting blue twilight that inspired so many great artists. Warm for early spring, Thierry shrugged off his leather jacket. He was tall and slim with jet-black hair and a classic Gallic nose - his handsome face marred whenever he smiled, revealing crooked, nicotine-stained teeth. He gazed across the street as shadows crept up the marble façade of his ancestral home, now the Picasso Museum. Music spilled from a nearby cafe as a chic neighborhood woman waited for her small dog to finish shitting on the pavement.

He spat in disgust at both the dog and his lost heritage. The only benefits of being of noble birth in France were ignominy and destitution. He drew out a blue envelope of Gitanes tobacco and deftly rolled a cigarette as the middle-aged woman crossed the street, dragging the small dog behind her. At least she had nice legs. With a shrug, he turned and strode down the sidewalk, flicking his lighter to life. He was late for his father, who waited around the corner in his flat on Rue Vielle du Temple.

Punching in the security code, he pushed open the door of the three-hundred-year-old building. A covered walkway led to an airy space enclosed by stone walls once used to house horses. High windows looked down on the empty courtyard and overflowing trash bins. He ran up the steep, curving staircase to the third floor. Water stains on the carpet indicated another pipe had burst somewhere. Thierry had argued with his aging father about moving to a more comfortable and accessible place. But Roger refused to leave his beloved Marais district, where he still felt close to the forgotten glory of his ancestors. Regardless of their tumultuous relationship, he preferred to be near his father. After the death of his mother, Roger remained his only living relative, leaving Thierry with the dubious honor of being the last of the House of Aubert. The family had been in steady decline for over two hundred years.

The key slipped into the lock. Thierry expected his father's usual loud complaining, but only silence greeted him. The small apartment appeared unchanged – filled with expensive antiques and Roger's prized portrait of Émile Zola by Manet – but a foreboding sense of absence tingled Thierry's senses. His father had explicitly told him to arrive at six o'clock, as he had something important to discuss.

"Roger?" he called. "*Papa*, are you here?"

Unwashed dishes filled the sink. The bed was unmade, gauzy curtains still drawn shut. A valuable old leather-bound book lay open on the Persian rug, spine cracked. Nearby, an unfamiliar satellite phone rested on the marble-topped table beside a parchment paper note. A man's severed finger wearing Roger Aubert's gold family crest ring rested in his father's priceless celadon-green Chinese jade bowl.

Thierry wrenched open the stiff paper and read: *Interpol is listening. Take the phone to the park behind Notre Dame.*

Ears buzzing with panic, he stormed from the apartment. The district's distinctive buildings reared on either side, but fury blinded him as he ran toward the Seine. At the cathedral, he scanned for watchers. Anyone could be behind the abduction, but he had a good idea. Maurice Costa's *Brise de Mer* Corsican mafia was known for dismembering their enemies.

Thierry had repeatedly warned his father of the risk of partnering with such a man. Not a man, but an animal – a shark who only existed to eat smaller fish. Had greedy Roger stolen from the king of thieves himself?

Thierry took several calming breaths, just another attractive young man on a bench watching people and pigeons. With the bulky phone in his lap his eyes tracked the edges of the park, the lines of the church, for anything unusual. He rolled another cigarette, lit up, and inhaled blue smoke. A young child cried out for his mother to push him on the swing. Minutes passed like the time it took for a mountain to wash to the sea.

The phone rang. "Are you there?" A voice demanded in Corsu, the French dialect of Corsica. "Your fool of a father's apartment is under surveillance."

"Where is Roger?"

"He is alive. For now. We have a job for you," said the man, his harsh voice and raspy grate that of a lifelong smoker. "We want you to go back to Burma. There's been a sighting of the Heart Stone ruby."

Shocked at the proposition, Thierry ground his cigarette into the dirt with his foot. "You know it can't be done. The country is a police state with eyes everywhere."

The man's sandpaper breath grated in his ear. "Do you want to see *cher papa* again?"

"Let me speak to Roger," he shouted. An old man feeding torn baguettes to the pigeons turned to look.

"Calm down, my boy. I know you've been searching for the stone, and now you will find it. It's simple – the old man for the gem, plus a hefty commission. And you will have the help of my contact. He's an old friend of yours." Costa chuckled with a deep, phlegmy sound that had nothing to do with mirth. "It will be a wonderful reunion."

"How long have you been watching me?" Thierry hissed into the receiver.

"You'd better get moving. *L'Anglais* is waiting," the gangster said.

Birds scattered up into the sky at the sound of the phone shattering on the cobblestones. The child on the swing regarded him with enormous eyes. The mother pulled the boy off the seat and, holding his little hand, marched toward the exit gate, perk ass twisting, high heels clicking on the slate gray stones.

CHAPTER THREE

Mallory

The scritch, scritch sound of palm trees outside Mallory's window woke her from a paralytic jet-lagged sleep. The fronds rubbing together made a noise that was driving her crazy. Her travel alarm clock read 7:39. But morning or night? The thirteen-and-a-half-hour time difference was mind-numbing. And how can a time zone be measured in half-hour increments? She counted backward with her fingers. Right now, she would be in the midst of the first rush of evening dinner reservations. She'd been managing restaurants for years and knew her way around a kitchen better than her own body. But setting up a new business venture in a foreign country? Laying on the soggy sheets, the enthusiasm that had fueled her decision to come to Burma melted away. With a groan, she rolled off the bed.

After a cold shower and an unsatisfactory cup of coffee, she rallied. No more moping about. Mallory was hired to manage a project, and her new boss would want an update. Her guidebook was light on details about the hospitality industry in Burma, but before leaving, she'd read what she could find at the Seattle library. For decades, the government had closed all the windows and doors and put out a closed sign. But her new employer had promised things were different. The open-for-business sign was turned on and flashing. She tried not to panic that he hadn't replied to her arrival fax. He was probably busy. It would all be okay. Besides, she couldn't go back.

At reception, Cho Cho wrote the word *bookstore* in Burmese on a bit of paper. Apologizing that there were no on-demand taxis, she suggested Mallory might walk to the boulevard and flag one down. She pressed an old umbrella into Mallory's hands. "Handy for rain or to keep the dogs away."

"Dogs?"

"Yes, Miss. Many dogs in Burma."

Beyond the hotel's long driveway, the road meandered down a hill lush with palms, drooping mango trees, and houseplants grown ridiculously huge. No animals chased her, but she almost fell several times on the sidewalk, skate-rink slippery with monsoon debris. Shrill birds called to one another across the treetops as insects churred a blanket of sound. One unseen bird caught her attention, the call coming from far away, sounding poignant and alone.

Mallory arrived at the boulevard sweaty yet exhilarated by the small accomplishment. But the excitement fizzled as she stood beside the road, watching impossibly crowded buses roar past. After long minutes, a tiny blue taxi stopped, and a grizzled man with white hair and betel-stained red teeth asked, "Where you go?"

"Downtown?" She clambered into the back.

Years of British colonial rule had left Rangoon with gracious boulevards and an organized grid street plan. Still, the capital city's infrastructure had suffered terrible neglect in the thirty-three years since Burma's independence. Viridescent ribbons of mold streaked every surface. The liquid heat and faded facades enhanced the impression of grand architecture melting into decay.

Her driver stopped before the Innwa Government Bookstore, a once stately two-story white-washed building. Mallory climbed out of the mini truck taxi, holding out several of the kyat notes she'd exchanged at the hotel. With a grin, the man grabbed a pink five hundred note and sped off. Displayed heaps of magazines and moldering paperbacks crowded the sidewalk in front of the shop. Tip-toeing around the piles, Mallory entered the black maw of an entrance. The electricity was out.

"Do you have books in English on doing business in Burma?" she asked an older man seated behind a wooden counter.

Obviously delighted to have a potential customer, he slipped off his stool and shuffled toward her. "We have plenty. Please take a look." He beckoned her to a table near the shadowy rear of the store and handed her a hardbacked book that smelled of mildew. A slippery insect with long antennae sped across the page as she opened it. The man chuckled nervously. "Silverfish like books very much."

"Do you have anything more recent?" The book had been published in 1952.

The man's smile shifted. "No, I'm afraid not." His shoulders rose and fell in a *what can you do* gesture. "No private business since government coup in 1962."

But it was 1995, and the country was supposed to be wide open, welcoming new ventures. The government needed the hard currency of foreign investment. Mallory stood outside the bookshop, uncertain of what to do next. At home, she would talk to other restaurant managers or go to the local chamber of commerce. Did Rangoon even have business associations? Most people passed by with smiles and nods, but some shot dark stares and walked around her as if she might contaminate them with her foreignness. They'd probably kick her out of the country if they knew the truth.

"Minglaba! Where you come from?" asked a blushing teenager, prompted by her giggling friends. The four school girls wore green longyi with white cotton tops, their long hair in braids or held back with ribbons.

"I come from America," Mallory said, relieved by their happy excitement. "What are you eating?" She pointed to the small plastic bag one of the girls was holding.

The girl's eyes went wide with alarm at the direct question. She looked to her friend for help. "Pancake," said the friend. "Very delicious. You like?"

An animated discussion ensued that Mallory guessed had to do with whether or not to offer Mallory a bite. Consensus reached, the English-speaking girl took her hand. "Come, we show you."

Near the end of the block, a street vendor had set up under a makeshift shelter – a tarp suspended over his mobile kitchen to protect from sun and rain. He grinned at the arrival of the school girls towing Mallory like a trophy. His betel-stained teeth and greasy ponytail didn't inspire confidence, but the girls didn't hesitate to place an order. Grabbing a ladle, he poured batter over a hot griddle with the expertise of a Michelin-starred chef. Her stomach growled in anticipation as the pancake bubbled and steamed. After a few moments, he flipped it over, revealing a crispy brown surface.

"You like egg?" asked the English speaker. The sight of the fluffy pancake removed any doubt about eating on the sidewalk. With a nod, the cook quickly fried an egg, placed it on top, and rolled up the treat. The first bite was as delicious as she'd hoped - a Burmese Egg McMuffin extraordinaire.

As she devoured the first good meal since her arrival, Mallory fielded questions from the school girls about Madonna and other celebrities she might have met. The girls' sweet naivety – assuming Mallory was someone who hung out with the famous just because she was American – charmed her. But soon, late for afternoon classes, the girls flew off like sparrows, leaving Mallory alone, wiping her greasy fingers on her skirt.

She began to walk toward the river, stepping across open drains and broken sidewalks. A sudden shower emptied the street of pedestrians. Mallory continued, welcoming the warm rain taking the edge off the heat. One foot before the other, like walking through several feet of water. With a start, she noticed people watching her from doorways and windows as if a spotlight followed her, signaling her out as different. Not only because she was strolling like a fool in the downpour, but they watched for something else, something unsettling.

Suddenly, the school girls' giggling questions didn't seem so sweet. Mallory's back tingled from the stares. Three young men huddling on their haunches in a sheltered doorway went silent as she passed. A beggar woman cradling a baby to her breast held out a hand with fingers eaten away by leprosy. Finally, another taxi stopped. Back in her air-conditioned room, she stretched out on the narrow bed, shivering in her rain-damp clothes, kicking herself for being a gullible fool. She may have escaped a bad situation back home only to land in something worse. Out of the proverbial frying pan into the fire.

The job posting in *Seattle Weekly Magazine*'s help-wanted section had been light on details but intriguing. *Motivated Executive Chef wanted for an international restaurant project. Generous salary, living expenses, autonomy.* Well, Mallory was motivated, all right. Desperate even. Thirty-three years old with an empty bed, bank account, and future. The first time she'd dialed, no one picked up. The hiccup of a ringtone was strange, and she imagined the phone ringing in a forlorn office on another planet.

But the second time, a polite man with an English accent answered.

CHAPTER FOUR

Thierry

Why was the bread in Asia so repugnant? Thierry found Burma disgusting for many reasons, but especially the cuisine. The Frenchman crushed his lit cigarette into the runny eggs on his plate and pushed away the cup of what the waiter had called coffee. Late-season monsoon thundered outside the window but did little to cool the dining room's temperature. His contact was late. He wondered if his father was still alive or if all his other body parts had been sliced into bits and fed to Maurice Costa's hungry pigs.

The Winner Inn was a converted two-story home set back from busy Inya Road. Like most of the houses in Rangoon, iron security bars fronted the windows and doors. Decorative design work did little to diminish the similarity to a prison. He hated the thought of being locked in a room with no chance of escape. A friend had recommended the place for its central location and fair price, but Thierry regretted the choice already.

"No more," he waved away the eager waiter who attempted to bring him another cup of coffee. "But, take this plate before I am sick." Thierry pushed his rattan chair back from the table. The downpour stopped, and the air conditioning finally began to dent the turgid atmosphere. The other breakfast guests left, and the room was his. He reached to the floor and pulled up the leather portfolio containing his notes.

Two years before, Thierry had learned about the Heart Stone ruby at a gemology conference in Bangkok. Expensive jewels were often deceptive fakes, and a professional thief needed the expertise to recognize the difference. The presenter had passed around a counterfeit jewel the size of a quail egg as an example. The forgery was of a legendary ruby first mentioned in thirteenth-century scrolls depicting Kublai Khan's invasion of the kingdom of Pagan – now Burma.

Thierry had held the facsimile up to the light, his fingers trembling with the memory of a story from his family's history. In the 1880s, his ancestor, Laurence Aubert, had traveled to Burma on behalf of Napoleon III to trade guns for gems. Laurence reportedly returned to France with tales of fist-sized gems, but no deal. Thierry stood in the middle of that Bangkok conference room, captured in a fairytale of the past and potential for the future, determined to find the real ruby.

He had visited Burma twice, following clues, and would gladly drink all the bad coffee in the world to find the famous gemstone he believed to be hidden somewhere in the country. What a thrill that would be to hold it in his palm and feel its ancient heart grow warm. And now – after a rumor was whispered in a Corsican gangster's ear – it had been found. But the gangster wanted it for himself and held his father as leverage.

"May I bring you anything, sir?" The young waiter hovered and then fled from Thierry's glare.

Outside the window, the downpour restarted. He picked up his father's family crest ring and slipped it on his finger. The only item of value left of *La Famille Aubert*, a worthless seven-hundred-year-old name. With barely contained fury, he tore open a packet of cigarettes.

He had to find that stone.

CHAPTER FIVE

Mallory

She was certainly on her own now, Mallory mused as she chewed on her fingertips, waiting for breakfast to be served. She would happily kill someone for a decent cup of coffee. After her adventure downtown the previous day, prickly heat had sprouted under her arms and between her thighs. A copy of Martin's most recent fax – received while still in Seattle – was tattered from rereading. At least she had the money. The only other guests in the dining room were a tall man in a shiny, tight suit with a heavy Russian accent and a tan Italian man in tennis shorts with a metal briefcase at his feet. They looked like extras from a spy movie.

Martin Payne was indeed British but lived and worked in Hong Kong. He managed an investment group that planned to open a restaurant in Rangoon, Burma. The employment application had appeared simple enough. Past executive chef-level management experience. References. Twelve-month contract with a year-to-year renewal option. Was she interested? He would provide additional details. She readily gave him the fax number of the restaurant where she worked, not caring if her boss noticed.

She'd been working as head chef for over three years with the empty promise of the general manager position dangled before her like a carrot. But her disgust for the restaurant owner had grown until she didn't know if she could wait any longer. She had to quit before she did something stupid.

Mallory's roommate, Liz, was shocked to learn Mallory planned to move to the other side of the world. "Are you insane? How can you trust these guys?"

Maybe I can't, Mallory thought. How can you trust anyone?

If Mallory's feasibility report received the green light from his group, Martin had explained, the architect and building contractor they used for past regional projects would come to oversee construction. The salary was more than she'd ever earned. When a package arrived with a plane ticket to Rangoon and an envelope filled with fifty crisp one-hundred-dollar bills, she'd ruffled the notes like a tiny book, inhaling the inky perfume of wealth. Packing her life into two suitcases had been remarkably easy.

***

"Good morning, Miss Mallory." Cho Cho stood by her table, looking fresh as a cucumber. "May I join you?"

"Sure."

"Are you enjoying our city?"

Mallory shrugged. "It's a bit overwhelming."

Cho Cho perched on the edge of a chair. "Perhaps I can be of assistance? Transportation can be challenging in the city without a car. My friend's husband could work for you as a driver."

Mallory sat back in surprise. "Does he speak English?"

"His English is not so good. But…" The young woman took a deep breath. "You might consider hiring me as your assistant?"

Cho Cho went on to explain that her salary at the hotel was the equivalent of forty dollars a month. A driver would expect a little more for the use of his car, plus gas. A salary paid in US dollars would be a significant bonus for them. Mallory understood the importance of a good crew; she'd hired and fired more than her fair share of workers. But without knowing the project's final budget, she hesitated.

At that moment, the young man who served as both the waiter and room cleaner set a plate of watery eggs and soggy white toast before her. From previous experience, Mallory knew the bread tasted like chalk.

"Do you not like the food here?" Cho Cho remarked as Mallory pushed away the dish.

"Actually, it's kind of bland."

"The cook assumed Westerners don't want to eat our local food."

"I'm a chef, so of course I want to sample the local cuisine." The memory of yesterday's pancake made her stomach grumble.

"Would you like to try something else?" That morning's leaf design on Cho Cho's cheeks gave the impression she'd just slipped out from a fairy-tale forest. Something about the sweet young woman inspired confidence.

"That would be great." Mallory made a snap decision. "And you're hired."

Cho Cho clapped her hands. "And Edward, the driver?"

"Him, too."

Cho Cho called the server and spoke animatedly in Burmese. Turning back to Mallory, she said, "It won't take long. I sent him to a noodle shop just down the street."

"Can we invite the driver for breakfast, too? I want to meet him."

"I will tell him to come, but he will be uncomfortable eating with us."

"Because I'm a foreigner?"

"No, because you have more status."

Status. Mallory rolled the word on her tongue like a piece of candy. She was glad there wasn't a mirror handy because she knew she wouldn't recognize the woman in the reflection.

As she waited for her second breakfast of the morning, a table was set up in the garden - the heat wasn't so uncomfortable in the shade. Cho Cho moved back and forth, bringing dishes and utensils. The young server came running up the drive, holding bulging plastic bags held aloft in victory.

"You will like this, I think," Cho Cho said as she emptied the contents into various bowls. "*Ohn no kauk swe* is a mild noodle dish made with coconut milk."

A fragrant cloud of steam encompassed Mallory's face as she peered into a bowl of thick, creamy broth. "This looks wonderful." She took a slurping bite of noodles and laughed as the broth dribbled down the front of her blouse. Everything was better after a decent meal. "After breakfast, can you take me to a local market so I can see what kinds of foodstuffs are available?"

"Sure, boss." Cho Cho grinned. "There is one not far from here."

***

The expansive wet market stood under an open-sided tin roof, with crowded aisles between wooden tables loaded with varied foodstuffs. Mounds of vividly colored fruit and vegetables stretched along the walkway, some familiar and others wildly exotic.

"What are those?" Mallory pointed at a chest-high pyramid of bright pink objects shaped like overgrown cactus grenades.

"That is *nagar ahmahthee*, dragon fruit," Cho Cho said.

The vendor, squatting on the ground with a towel wrapped around her head, grabbed one of the grenade fruits and deftly sliced it open, revealing a white interior speckled with tiny black seeds. She handed a piece to Mallory. The flavor was surprising – more kiwi-tart than the bubblegum-sweet the pink color implied. Familiar shallots, garlic, and small brown pota-toes overflowed from dusty baskets inside the market. Bags of ground turmeric and coriander spiced the air; mountains of greens, tied into bundles, wilted in the heat.

Strolling through the plentitude, Mallory imagined rework-ing tried and true recipes with the local ingredients. Recipes were dependable friends, but the strange fruit and vegetables fired her imagination. She desperately wanted a new kitchen to experiment with Rangoon's intriguing blend of familiar and exotic. Cooking was part chemistry and part magic, and Mallory was a skilled magician.

After a short time, the heat spawned a pungent sauna under the metal roof, and the profound stench caused her eyes to water. In the fish section, a girl scraped the body of an iri-descent fish with an iron knife. A woman in a blue and green striped longyi haggled over a plastic bag of pink shrimp. A bucket of live eels tumbled over each other.

Deeper into the market, the concrete flooring became dirt. Chickens in woven bamboo cages squawked in fear. Fat flies swarmed glistening skinned carcasses hanging from rusty hooks while a cleaver-wielding man in a white skull cap chopped at the ribs of an unfamiliar animal. Goat? Sheep? Mallory had butchered her fair share of beasts, but this was too much. Her delicious breakfast threatened to join the mess on the ground.

She signaled to Cho Cho—time to go. Stumbling over uneven ground, she fled into the waiting car. "Take me back to the hotel," she told Edward as Cho Cho slid onto the seat beside her.

CHAPTER SIX

Geoffrey Hughes

Geoffrey nodded to the dignified doorman sporting an elegant Shan jacket. A Burmese musician played the patala as he entered the foyer of the Strand Hotel, the bamboo xylophone's notes pattering like gentle rain. The Englishman stopped to breathe in the sweet fragrance of fresh-cut flowers gracing a carved antique table. His hunched shoulders relaxed as he took several steps and turned right into Sarkies Bar. He loved everything about the historic Strand Hotel –especially Friday nights.

Built by two Armenian brothers in 1901, the Strand was one of the most luxurious hotels of the former British Empire. Geoffrey could imagine himself in the company of the famous writers who had stayed there: Orwell, Somerset Maugham, Kipling. The hotel had been renovated as a beautiful testament to the past and was his favorite place in the city.

Friday night's Happy Hour was the one permanent appointment on his social calendar. Not Paris, but it would do in a pinch. He was steeped in the Strand's checkered history, like a cup of fragrant Earl Grey tea. But it wasn't history that enticed him each week at seven o'clock. It was gossip and the latest drunken dramas in his small European Rangoon-based community.

The long bar resembled a Victorian gentleman's club with polished teak wainscoting and over-stuffed leather armchairs. Obsequious waiters wore white jackets with black bow ties. Faded sepia photographs of an era long gone hung on the walls. A trio of ancient Burmese men in dusty tuxedos played 1930s jazz standards in the corner. Cigarette and cigar smoke drifted up to the rattan ceiling fans.

With Tanqueray and tonic in hand, he surveyed the crowded room from his usual spot at the polished bar while keeping an eye on the new bartender with the gorgeous long eyelashes. Geoffrey loved young men with long eyelashes. In fact, the same sort of young man had been responsible for exiling him to this remote diplomatic outpost in the first place. The Queen didn't like Her Majesty's Foreign Service servants to embarrass the Crown. And Geoffrey had been a very bad boy.

An unfamiliar young woman stood in the doorway – he noticed her immediately. She had a translucent complexion with bronze-hued shoulder-length hair. He imagined blue veins under the skin at her wrists. She wore a simple linen shift emphasizing her slim figure and bright vermillion lipstick. Heads turned, and one man literally licked his lips as he followed her progress across the room.

Fresh meat for the sharks.

Geoffrey pushed aside his colleague from the British consulate and waved her over. "Sit here, my dear."

"Thank you," she said. "This is quite a crowd."

The bartender hurried over to take her order for a glass of house white wine. "Put that on my account," Geoffrey said.

"You don't need to do that."

The woman was even prettier than at first glance, her eyes an unusual shade of witchy green. How delightful. Geoffrey adored beauty above all else. "My pleasure. We don't have many visitors like you."

"What do you mean, like me?"

Just then, a heavyset Australian man pushed up between

them to order and took the opportunity to brush against the woman. "Sorry, love. Can I buy you a drink?" The Aussie's eyes scanned her body.

"No thanks. But you could get yourself a life."

At a loss for words, the Aussie laughed good-naturedly and lightly punched her arm. "Tell me when you're bored with the poofter."

"Better get accustomed to that," Geoffrey said, following the man with narrowed eyes. "Unfortunately, most men become complete idiots when they're here, away from wifey back home."

"What about the women?"

"Well, a Western woman only comes here to find a husband, and after she gets pregnant,   he ships her safely home."

"You're not serious!"

"Of course not, you noodle." He picked up his packet of Benson & Hedges. "Cigarette?" She shook her head no. He flicked his lighter and took a deep inhale. "Please don't be offended," he spoke through a plume of smoke. "I'm blessed with an irreverent sense of humor that gets me into terrible trouble."

The bartender set a glass of wine and a bowl of spiced peanuts before the woman. "Thank you." She nodded to both the barman and Geoffrey. She took a sip and made a sour face.

"Here, let me order you something decent." He instructed the young man to bring the lady a glass of Geoffrey's usual white. "It takes time to learn which wines can handle the heat here. The Sancerre is palatable, but you're better off with whisky or gin."

"Who in the world are you?"

"Geoffrey Hughes." He took a slight bow. "I'm with the British Consulate. Now, please tell me, what is a pretty American like you doing in this backwater of damaged souls, and why haven't we yet met?"

She laughed aloud. "My name is Mallory Jones, and I'm here opening a restaurant."

"Thank God, how marvelous. There are so few spots for a decent meal. What type of cuisine and where will it be located?"

"I'm still figuring it out. It will probably be some sort of east-west fusion. I want to incorporate local ingredients. I would love to find a colonial-era space to renovate, but I'm finding the owners of the old buildings impossible to track down. There are loads of beautiful places, and I love the history, but they're in such bad shape. I came here tonight for some inspiration."

Geoffrey smiled. Helping the young woman would be a welcome and entertaining distraction from his other, more worrisome activities. Leaning forward, he squeezed her elbow. "I have an amazing broker. Jenny knows absolutely everybody and is extremely well-connected. Connections are critical here."

The barman arrived with the replacement glass of wine. The woman took a sip and then an impressive swallow. She nodded her approval, smiling with her curious eyes. "Any help would be welcome – and you're right about the Sancerre. Now, what do you mean by 'backwater of damaged souls'? That's a little extreme, isn't it?"

"Oh, you'll soon learn. Most everyone here is damaged in some way – the European business expats, at least. They can't succeed at home and come here to be big fish in a small pond."

"Guess I'll fit right in," she said, a shadow crossing her face.

Geoffrey signaled for another round of drinks. He'd only recently reconciled his own particular damage. Coming from an upper-class background and all the privilege that entailed, he had thrown it all away for nothing. He glimpsed himself in the bar mirror and cringed at his big nose, pouchy eyes, and yellow complexion. He'd once been handsome, but the man in the reflection was old and pitiful.

He swiveled toward the American woman's beauty as if to

the sun. "We each have our dirty little secrets, don't we?"

With a grimace for a smile, he gulped down his remaining gin.

CHAPTER SEVEN

Mallory

Cho Cho's formal tone indicated having guests wasn't a regular occurrence. Her grandparents, U Hlaing and Daw Sein, lived in the northern Rangoon township of Okkalapa. The narrow concrete apartment block rose like a tower, surrounded by a village neighborhood of unpaved roads and wooden huts where people spent their lives in the open. Dinner was early by Mallory's standards, but she was grateful for the remaining daylight as she followed her assistant up four flights of a narrow, grimy staircase.

The old couple waited at the apartment door entrance, looking like mismatched bookends—one short and one tall. After welcoming handshakes and removal of shoes, Mallory entered the modest home.

"Please be seated," U Hlaing said. "We have been waiting for you." The old man's educated formality stood in stark contrast to his humble surroundings.

A large dining table covered with servings of food dominated the dim room. The only daylight came from the sliding door to a tiny outdoor terrace engulfed by potted plants.

"I'm sorry if we're late," Mallory said.

"No, no, you are right on time. Please be seated." Daw Sein, U Hlaing's apple-shaped wife hovered, her hands twisted with nervousness. "We prepared a proper Burmese meal. Our granddaughter told us you are a chef from America, interested in learning about our food traditions." Without pausing for a reply, she pointed to various bowls. "It must consist of different tastes – sweet, bitter, salty, astringent, and sour – each touching a different part of the palette."

"I'm looking forward to this," Mallory said. "I like learning new recipes."

Mallory was about twelve when she discovered Irma Rombauer's *Joy of Cooking* at the bottom of a 'for free' box at the local church bazaar. The torn and stained cookbook, with its magic potion recipes, provided her an escape better than TV or movies. And best of all, her grumpy foster parents didn't complain when she placed a casserole of made-from-scratch mac and cheese or still-warm apple pie on the dinner table. She spent her time after school practicing, striving to create the perfect dish to sustain her starving spirit.

A single light illuminated the feast with a chiaroscuro effect. U Hlaing sat at the head of the table and his granddaughter across. Cho Cho's grandmother continued with a gentle teacher's tone. "We soothe our hunger with rice and our appetite with these flavors." She spooned fragrant white rice on Mallory's plate and then added a bit from each small bowl. "Try a bite of each, and then tell me your favorite."

Mallory took a nibble of prawn cooked in a spicy tomato curry. It was silent except for the sound of chewing and the clink of spoons. Tender morning glory greens sautéed with garlic, followed by grilled eggplant with raw onions soaked in fragrant oil. There was no wine, only a pungent, sour soup with bitter greens to wash it down. Daw Sein sat at her guest's side, monitoring the never-empty plate.

"You are a remarkable cook," Mallory said later, unable to eat another bite.

Daw Sein blushed. "But we are not finished yet," she said. "We must eat *laphet thouk*."

Cho Cho brought a bowl of oranges and a round lacquered dish separated into five wheel-like sections with a space at the center for pickled tea leaves soaked in peanut oil. Various crispy fried foods and nuts filled the 'spokes' of the wheel.

U Hlaing demonstrated the correct eating technique. "Like this, make a small scoop with two fingers and your thumb, and pick up a bit of the tea leaf." Certain she would make a mess, Mallory guided a sesame seed-embedded dollop into her mouth.

"Are you homesick?" Cho Cho asked. "I can't imagine being so far from my family."

Mallory chuckled at the thought of missing her family. Homesickness was an unfamiliar concept to someone who had never known a home. Seattle seemed small and far away, like viewing the wrong end of a telescope. "No, I'm not homesick," she said. "I hope Burma will be my new home."

"We want to thank you for giving our granddaughter employment," U Hlaing said.

"I was lucky to meet you at the airport. I'm usually not very lucky." Mallory tapped the necklace she wore for special occasions in a gesture like throwing salt over one's shoulder or touching wood.

"Your ruby is lovely. Where did it come from?" Daw Sein leaned forward for a better look.

"I doubt it's real; it was my mother's. She died when I was little."

"May I see?" Daw Sein held out her hand.

"Ruby or glass, the memory of your mother makes the necklace precious," U Hlaing said. "Cho Cho lost both her parents in a terrible accident when she was very young. Certainly, a tragedy for us all, but it brought us together in a way we might not otherwise have known." He looked at his granddaughter with such tenderness a flicker of jealousy passed through Mallory. "Are you close with your father?" he asked.

"No, he's dead, too." Her tone didn't invite any further questioning.

The emotion was as fresh as the orange peel on her fingertips. The excitement when the policewoman with the heavy gun on her belt had come into Mallory's second-grade classroom to take her home early. The taste of the lollipop she'd given Mallory as they sat in her cruiser waiting for the social worker. *Terrible accident. So sorry to tell you. A nice lady will take you to her house for a little while until arrangements can be made.* The look on the policewoman's face when little Mallory began to laugh.

Mallory's father had been driving drunk and crashed into a garbage truck, surviving with nothing more than a seatbelt bruise and a verdict of vehicular manslaughter. Her mother was thrown from the car and died on impact, her head smashed like an egg.

But Mal had fixed all that. *Bye-bye, Daddy.*

Mallory tore the peel from the orange and popped the sweetness into her mouth. Delicious. Night pressed against the window as Cho Cho moved about the room, lighting kerosene lamps to augment the dim bulb.

U Hlaing leaned forward, earnest in his expression. "How much do you know about our country?"

"Not much, I guess," Mallory said. "What I could find in the library and what my new employer told me. And, of course, *The Lonely Planet* guidebook," she smiled. "It's been very helpful."

"Please know, we pray your restaurant will be successful. But Burma has been a closed economy for a long time. Other than your project, only a few multi-national hotel companies are investing here." U Hlaing's weary sigh encompassed the past three decades. "There are rumors of corruption and money laundering at the highest level."

Mallory knew a little about the endemic cronyism spoiling the dictatorship's economy. "Don't you think it's improving by allowing outside investment?"

He shook his head in frustration. "We have two different economies: the official and the black market. The official exchange rate is about six kyats to one US dollar. Our people are paid on the assumption of that value. But everyone uses the black-market rate of one hundred kyats to one dollar. The authorities overlook it and become rich in the shadows. People are very private about their affairs here. They don't want the attention of the government. I don't wish to alarm you, but you must be very cautious."

Cho Cho lowered her voice as if the walls could hear. "Also, many people are afraid of being caught speaking against the generals. People who talk to foreigners are especially watched. My grandparents had to get approval for your visit and must file a report tomorrow with the local township authority."

"It sounds like living in the Soviet Union or something."

"It became even worse after the uprising a few years ago," said Cho Cho.

"Our country was destroyed," Daw Sein added.

"What happened?" Mallory said.

"Our leader's fortune-teller told him that nine was his lucky number and would protect him from his enemies," U Hlaing said. "The general switched the currency from multiples of ten to those of nine, printing ninety kyat and forty-five-kyat bills to replace the one-hundred-fifty note denominations."

"How can someone arbitrarily replace money?" Mallory imagined twenty-dollar bills morphed into the currency she'd had to purchase upon arrival, her five-thousand-dollar advance reduced to nothing.

"He also declared all the former denominations to be worthless, so many people became penniless overnight," Daw Sein added.

"We lost all our wealth." Daw Sein spoke in a low voice. "We had to sell our beautiful home in Golden Valley and move to this small apartment."

Mallory understood being poor – having to slice green mold from the corner of the last piece of Wonder bread. Poverty stained for life.

"A very bad time," U Hlaing said. "Especially for our youth. Many demonstrated against the government. They were so hopeful, certain they would finally make a change. They marched with signs and banners. But the police beat them until the streets flowed with blood. Then they closed all the universities."

"I wanted to be a doctor," Cho Cho whispered. "Have a family."

Daw Sein put her hand on top of Mallory's. "We pray that General Ne Win and his cronies will relax their iron rule. Perhaps now, they are. For why else would you be here, Miss Mallory?" Quiet settled around the table. Mallory had no reply suitable to soothe the ache in her new friends' voices. "Excuse me for a moment." Daw Sein shuffled out of the room.

Mallory stiffened as she realized the woman had taken her mother's necklace with her. But Daw Sein returned holding a jeweler's loupe and the necklace. "Are you a jeweler on the side?" Mallory joked, uneasy having someone examine the pendant so closely. The past was off-limits.

Cho Cho stood next to her grandmother, taking a turn to look into the red depths. "Many Burmese keep their wealth in jewels. We are all experts now." She handed Mallory the loupe.

Mallory held the eyepiece to her mother's necklace. "Is it real?" A surge of unfamiliar hope bloomed in her chest.

"No, it is not," Cho Cho said with a sad smile. "But it *is* a very lovely piece of glass."

Of course, it was fake – like everything else in her life.

CHAPTER EIGHT

Thierry

When Geoffrey Hughes filled the doorway, Thierry choked. He'd expected the contact to be Burmese, not someone he already knew. The last time he'd seen Geoffrey, he'd almost murdered the man. The Englishman had made the mistake of blackmailing him.

"What the hell are *you* doing here?"

"Won't you invite an old friend to sit? How was your breakfast?"

A terrible realization took shape. Not only did Geoffrey know about the ruby, he knew Costa and was involved with Roger's kidnapping. "Why are you here?" he repeated.

"One thing at a time. Perhaps we should have some privacy? The waiter who welcomed me seems nice, but one never knows."

Thierry scanned the dining room and, indeed, the young Burmese waiter loitered just outside the doorway. Thierry hated Geoffrey, but the man had a point. Anyone, anywhere in the wretched country, might be spying and reporting back to the intelligence service. At that moment, some scrawny bureaucrat was probably documenting that Thierry hadn't eaten all his breakfast. Fear framed the entire fabric of the nation. He imagined whole city blocks filled with warehoused reports. If the government heard a whisper of their plan to steal the Heart Stone, they would spend the rest of their lives rotting in prison – if not worse.

"Let's go up to my room."

"Whatever you say," Geoffrey smirked.

He led Geoffrey up wooden stairs to the second floor, mind ablaze as he unlocked the door. Had he heard a rumor that Geoffrey had been reassigned to Burma? He came up blank. Over two years since they'd last been in the same room, he felt a grim satisfaction that the vain Englishman wasn't aging well.

"How are you involved with all this?" Thierry asked.

"Let's tip-toe down memory lane, shall we?" Geoffrey sneered as he sat in the only chair. "You must remember Janice, the obscenely wealthy hag in Paris? I know you remember her dinner party in Saint Germaine des Pres?" Geoffrey took a packet of cigarettes from his shirt pocket. "Do you have a light?"

Throwing his lighter, Thierry barely missed Geoffrey's face. "And I know *you* remember that I almost killed you later."

"Cheers." Geoffrey lit his cigarette and took a deep drag. "I'll never forget that meal – oysters so fresh they winced, then beef tenderloin drizzled with cognac butter on a bed of crème fraîche-infused carrot mash. God, how I miss decent food."

"Get to the point."

Geoffrey continued as if he hadn't heard. "Ah, Janice. She had the best tits and ass money could buy, but your eyes were locked on nothing except those sapphires around her neck. For hours I sat across from you as you lusted after those stones." Geoffrey tapped his cigarette ash on the parquet floor. "And, as you know, a little birdie told me she'd been burgled a week later, that beautiful necklace stolen along with other valuable trinkets."

Of course, Thierry remembered the wealthy American

widow and that dinner. Shortly before the guests arrived, he'd fucked her wearing the jewels, all the while planning how to open the safe hidden under her Aubusson carpet. And then later, he'd met diplomat Geoffrey Hughes sitting across the white linen table, one of twenty glitterati guests guzzling Janice's vintage champagne, grinning and genuflecting before her wealth.

After the news about the jewelry theft made headlines in the Paris newspapers, Geoffrey tracked down Thierry and dared to blackmail him by threatening to tell the police about Thierry's relationship with Janice. He had quickly changed Geoffrey's mind with the sharp end of a knife. But Thierry still had to flee Paris until Janice received her hefty insurance check and lost interest in the entire affair.

"Does the scar still show?"

Geoffrey adjusted his silk cravat. "Only sometimes."

"Enough reminiscing. Now, how do you know about the ruby and Maurice Costa?"

"Well, Maurice and I are old friends, you might say," Geoffrey blew a perfect smoke ring. "We've done business in the past. And you would never have come to Rangoon if I'd asked sweetly, would you? I needed someone with a bit stronger...shall we say...influence, to entice your help."

"So, you had my father maimed and kidnapped? Why me? There are many thieves."

"Maimed?" The Englishman raised his eyebrows. "Listen, you're perfect for this. I know you're already obsessed with this particular gem. I happened to be in the right place at the right time to receive a bit of gossip, which I shared with our mutual friend. I can't do this alone, and that's where a thug like Costa comes in handy. You won't risk cheating me if your father's health is, shall we say, at risk?"

Thierry restrained himself from throwing the old man against the wall. "Why should I believe you know the location? Why would a discredited old pédé like you know the secret location of an ancient priceless artifact?"

Geoffrey's mild expression transformed. "Well, precisely because I am who I am, you arrogant, small-minded ass-wipe of a gigolo." He threw the lighter back, striking Thierry's chest with a dull thud.

Thierry felt a flicker of fear – did he really know the man sitting across from him? But there was no time, no other choice. "Where is it?"

"I'll know soon." Geoffrey's face shifted back, the hatred dissolving like a wave washing the shoreline smooth. "You have to be patient for now."

Thierry's clenched jaw ached. "You realize I have to steal it, and then we have to smuggle it out of this damned military dictatorship?"

Geoffrey walked to the door. "Don't despair, mon garçon. I have an excellent plan."

After the Englishman's departure, Thierry remained seated on the side of the bed, elbows on knees. He imagined Roger wounded, suffering, trapped in a Corsican cellar adjacent to a squealing pig pen – but felt nothing. Where had things gone wrong for the culture that had produced the finest literature and art? The land of Michelin stars and haute couture? Everything elegant and sublime had been commercialized into garbage, especially that of his family. He had to escape these dingy confines, or he'd go mad. He needed a distraction.

***

The vast hall of the Myanmar Gems Emporium on Kaba Aye Pagoda Road left Thierry in a daze of desire. Smooth-skinned pearls, piles of rainbow-hued jade, and bright flashes of peridot, the color of springtime in Paris, spread before him in an orgy of perfection. Unlike people, jewels were honest. They never lie or fail to be any more or less than promised.

He paused, captured by a set of perfect oval-shaped violet

sapphires arranged on a velvet tray as if for a necklace. The merchant jumped at the sight of the foreigner and slid the glinting jewels from the cabinet.

"Please, sir. Very beautiful sapphire. No heat treatment, all natural."

"Yes, lovely. How much are you asking?" Thierry could resell such a collection back home and make a decent profit, even though the local faceting work was rough by international standards. A return to Paris empty-handed was unthinkable.

"For you, special price..." The ages-old selling gambit began. The short and round merchant resembled a bowling ball with his sparkling polyester shirt. "This sapphire best quality. Sir, look..." He held out a loupe to inspect the stones. "This once necklace for Queen Supaylat."

Bargaining was always the same, no matter the country: an imagined, poetic history, the beauty of the jewels and, then, the delicate dance around money. Thierry sighed, suddenly bored by the ritual. "I'm looking for a particular ruby. Very old."

The man deflated, realizing a sale was unlikely – but gossip was a welcome alternative. "Not old, but SLORC ruby upstairs in museum for looking. I take you?"

Thierry had read about the infamous stone discovered in 1990, measuring almost five hundred carats. Referred to as the SLORC ruby, in recognition of the government's official title – State Law and Order Restoration Council – several miners and a Mandalay brothel owner had concocted a scheme to steal the stone and smuggle it from the country. Burmese government agents captured the men in Chiang Mai, Thailand. The plotters were tried without a jury and disappeared – either executed or left to rot in the aptly named Insein prison.

"I didn't know public viewing was allowed. I would like to see it very much."

"Please come," the rotund man grinned. "My name U Win.

You not an Englishman?"

"No, I am French."

"Ah, pyin thit. Welcome, sir. May I know your name?"

"Thierry."

"Dreary?" U Win laughed at his poor pronunciation. "Better I call you Monsieur."

The Burmese merchant slid the sapphires back under the counter and locked the cabinet with a tiny brass key. Thierry searched the room for cameras. It would be easy to help one-self to the man's collection, like taking candy from a child. But he remembered the armed guards. He stepped back, allowing the man to lead him from the cavernous hall.

"We go up, Monsieur. I show you the most famous pat-tamya. That is word for ruby in my language..." the man rambled as they rode the elevator up to the fourth floor.

At the museum's reception counter, a young woman – her sweet face at odds with her stodgy gray uniform – blushed as she asked Thierry for the one-dollar entry fee and his passport. "All foreign guests must leave passports here, sir," she whispered. He couldn't tell if she was just painfully shy or embarrassed. "Please sign ledger and I give receipt."

After taking the flimsy chit of paper, Thierry turned to find U Win waiting, chatting with another guard. This one wore a white shirt instead of blue and a very professional pistol at his waist. Were there specially trained sentries on this level? U Win explained that the museum held the most valuable and unique specimens from the government's min-eral and gem collection. Thierry expected a hall similar to the British Museum, with its extensive compilation of dusty rocks in squeaky drawers. But he was delighted to find a chic, dark-ened room with illuminated displays that would be suitable in a Cartier shop on the Champs-Elysees.

"Nice, yes?" the merchant said. "Come, I show you the Nawata. Better name than SLORC ruby."

In the center of the room, a prominent display case beck-oned. A golf ball-sized nugget of saturated hue and silky red fluorescence rested on a simple dais behind bullet-proof glass. Thierry licked his lips. The rock was uncut, as if wrenched alive from its metamorphic bed, but still retained its intrinsic radiant purity. Almost five hundred carats, he calculated. But even with a skilled lapidarist, the visible inclusions would make it much smaller if faceted. Similar weight, but the Heart Stone had already been cut and polished. If the depictions in the portraits of Isabella of Spain and Catherine the Great of Russia were accurate, the finished jewel would be the size of the Nawata before him. Staggering for such a perfect specimen. His mouth went dry.

"From Mogok Valley." U Win appeared by his elbow.

"It is remarkable. But it is not the ruby I desire."

"What could be better than the Nawata?"

"There have been many names over the centuries, but I call it the Heart Stone." He took a deep breath. "A jewel that adorned royalty for a thousand years and is rumored to have originally come from the kingdom of Pagan in upper Burma."

U Win's eyes grew round. "Boddha Hnalonetha - the Buddha's Heart. But it is only legend."

"The legend may be true. What more can you tell me about it?"

"I tell you a story, but not here." The merchant swiveled his eyes to the guards in the unique way Burmese could see without turning their heads. "I close shop for lunchtime."

Downstairs from the museum, U Win asked a neighboring shopkeeper to watch his counter as he was going to lunch with the foreigner. As he began to lock up, one of the guards left his corner and walked toward them. Thierry's back tingled as they walked past the guard and out the entrance to the hall. Glancing back, the machine gun-armed man smiled.

Waiting for the official to retrieve Thierry's passport from the locker behind her, Thierry caught sight of a mural on the far wall. The painting depicted a scene from the past: an affluent Burmese man, perhaps a king, reclined on a cushioned settee, as a bearded foreigner in a black suit and tie sat below him on the floor. A smoldering nugget was perched on the ornate table between them. They appeared to be negotiating or discussing the jewel. The foreign man's tie was depicted as the French flag.

"Who is that?" he asked.

"Minister to King Mindon."

"And the man with him?"

U Win's face creased with a bright smile. "Ah, pyin thit trader. Frenchman, like you! Mindon crafty king. He talk with France, keep the English away. Early 1800s, British Raj war take control lower part of country. Burmese king in Mandalay want protect upper part. Maybe with French help. But no good, English Queen Victoria and her many cannon take all country in 1885."

For once, his father hadn't lied. The sharp knot in Thierry's chest softened. He hoped his father remained safe. Adjacent to the museum, a small restaurant catered to tourists with an English-language menu and frigid air conditioning. Thierry ordered the *French-type Coffee*. He sighed when the drink arrived in a glass with a pink straw and a layer of whipped cream.

The gem dealer happily roosted himself before a bowl of what looked like green tapioca worms floating in milk. "I tell you fable story my father tell me long time past." He swallowed a dripping bite. "Many centuries ago, King Anawrahta of Pagan want precious offering to dedicate new pagoda to Lord Buddha. He send most trusted monks on dangerous journey to find. Long ago people believe rubies get ripe in the earth, like fruit. After months of much suffering, a girl child appears and show monks secret cave in hidden part of the valley. She points and tells where to dig. They find Boddha Hnalonetha, perfect in all ways, shaped like heart of child. King Anawrahta put in the center of Shwesandaw pagoda to consecrate." The round man sucked up the remains of his tapioca and leaned back, one stubby leg over the other. "That story of most famous ruby, Boddha Hnalonetha."

"Where is it now?"

"I don't know, monsieur. Still in heart of pagoda?"

"I doubt that." Thierry didn't hold back the frustration in his voice. There were no clues in the fable for him. He was stuck with Geoffrey to find the ruby.

Another grinning museum guard watched as Thierry waited for a taxi.

CHAPTER NINE

Mallory

Downtown Rangoon was less intimating from the backseat of an air-conditioned car. Traffic police waved white-gloved hands in an indecipherable semaphore. Dense neighborhoods with blocks of hive-like apartments dripped laundry, bougainvillea, and mold from wrought-iron balconies. Mallory was beginning to appreciate the city's chaotic beauty.

Stepping out of the car in front of the British Consulate building – another relic from the grander days of empire – she felt like a film star.

"Don't you look delicious?" Geoffrey greeted her from the shade of the portico.

Her navy cotton dress was nothing special, but she had put on her Lancôme lipstick and the necklace. Real or not, it was her only jewelry. She'd invited Geoffrey and his broker friend for lunch, and she didn't know how formal an affair it might be. "You're not so bad yourself," she said. The Englishman wore his habitual Graham Greene-inspired tropical suit with a jaunty paisley silk cravat.

They strolled next door to the Strand Hotel for a classic high tea lunch of cucumber finger sandwiches, clotted cream with freshly baked scones, and a selection of tiny perfect cakes on a tiered stand. Though Mallory had invited him, Geoffrey insisted they order a bottle of champagne. After perusing the wine list, he snapped his fingers for the waiter to take his order.

"Isn't that rude?" Mallory whispered as the straight-backed man marched away to fetch their sparkling brut. She hated bullying of any kind.

"Not at all, my dear. You'll get the hang of it."

As she began to protest, a Burmese woman resembling a princess from a bygone era entered the dining room and floated across the black and white tiles to their table. She wore a bright-colored silk longyi with a semi-transparent eingyi dotted with dainty emerald buttons. Her raven-dark hair was piled on her head in a cylindrical tower – a diamond necklace glittered at her throat. Mallory looked down at her dress with regret.

"Jenny, my love, how wonderful to see you!" Geoffrey stood to air-kiss the older woman's cheeks. "Thank you for joining us. Meet my darling new friend, Mallory Jones."

Her smile was kind. "How do you do, Miss Jones."

The host materialized to hold out Jenny's chair. "Join us for a glass of bubbly?" Geoffrey said.

Since her arrival, Mallory had never seen a Burmese woman drink anything besides coffee or juice, so she was surprised when Jenny nodded yes. The host also appeared startled until Jenny skewered him with a stern look. Three crystal flutes and a silver ice bucket arrived. The cork made a gentle pop as the waiter opened it.

"Cheers to old and new friends," the regal woman toasted, then downed her glass.

"Bottom's up," Geoffrey laughed.

"Have you been a property broker long?" Jenny was eye-ing the cakes. "Please help yourself," Mallory said.

"Yes, I have." Jenny reached for one of the delicacies with a small fork. "I have such a sweet tooth; I must be careful about getting too fat." Her laugh was self-deprecating, but her tone implied she didn't worry about anything so trivial as her waistline. "I've been an agent for a long time. You see, I'm a widow and must support myself. It isn't easy for a woman like me."

"What do you mean?" Any woman with a painful past intrigued her.

"Well, I met and fell in love with a Muslim man of Indian descent when I was very young. Coming from a traditional Burmese family, my parents disowned me for marrying a kala."

"An epic tale worthy of Shakespeare," Geoffrey interjected.

"After General Ne Win's coup and only one year of marriage," Jenny continued, apparently accustomed to Geoffrey's comments, "most wealthy citizens of different ethnic heritages were forced from the country so he could loot their personal properties and bank accounts. My husband lost everything and soon died of a heart attack."

Mallory sipped her wine and imagined what it must have been like to have everything and then lose it. Jenny's jewelry glittered under the lights – how much had she lost if she still had those diamonds?

"In need of income, I became a real estate broker to my former upper-class school chums who now looked down their noses at me," Jenny spoke with a level voice, never sounding sorry for herself. "And, being a lonely widow has had certain advantages," she winked. "Is there more wine?"

"That's my girl!" Geoffrey proclaimed. "Let's do another bottle, shall we?"

"Yes, another bottle." Mallory had no idea how much the champagne cost. Hopefully, the promised expense account would materialize soon.

"Wake up over there and bring us another bottle of champers," Geoffrey said.

Slightly drunk from all the wine, Mallory leaned forward to examine Jenny's hair. She restrained herself from touching the elaborate hairstyle dotted like a Christmas tree with tiny orange flowers.

"Jenny, my beauty, you resemble one of those old sepia photographs," Geoffrey said, "of Burmese women smoking cheroot cigars with hair several meters long."

Jenny's laugh was surprisingly deep. "Oh, I'm an old-fashioned lady. In my time, it was considered desirable to have hair long enough to stand upon. The young ones today don't have the patience and can entice men in other ways."

"To enticing men!" Geoffrey tilted the second empty bottle into the ice bucket – or was it the third?

Thank God for Edward, waiting patiently nearby. The doorman clapped his hands, and the driver appeared like a magic trick to help Mallory wobble down the Strand Hotel's front steps. The entire drive home, his eyes watched her in the rearview mirror as if afraid she might be sick in the car. Back at the hotel, she waved away his help as she tottered to her room and collapsed on the bed.

Eight days already – waiting for word from Martin while watching mushrooms sprout on her leather shoes. Each evening, she swore she would return to Seattle the next day. But, then, every new morning, she would slurp rice noodles in spicy fish broth or swipe her plate with paratha and chickpea dal and give him just one more day.

Like her brain, the paper in her spiral notebook went mushy with humidity. Pressure from her ballpoint pen imprinted rune shapes as the ink bled. Her concept for the restaurant was more evident every day – the type of building, menu, how many staff – but her workbook sketches and lists had smudged into an impressionistic smear. She started smoking again after swearing to herself she wouldn't. The mirror reflected sunken eyes in bruised circles of sleeplessness. The goddamn clacking of the palm fronds outside her window was really driving her insane.

She imagined stealing the gardener's machete and hacking down the tree.

CHAPTER TEN

Geoffrey

The barrel-bellied proprietor wiped Geoffrey's plastic table with a dirty rag before setting down a tin kettle and a teacup. "What you want?"

"An ashtray and a large bottle of beer. What kind do you carry?"

"Only Mandalay beer, here."

Geoffrey would kill for a good pour of Guinness with perfect thick foam and a color as dark as a young man's eyes. "Bring the largest."

The restaurant was child-sized by Western standards. Geoffrey was reminded of a playhouse designed by his young niece back home in Sussex. Not that his shit of a brother had ever let him near her. Customers squatted on footstools placed alongside the sidewalk. With imagination, one could almost be reminded of a Paris bistro. But who was he fooling? He now lived in the humid armpit of the world. He swallowed the bitter memory of Paris as he ducked under the torn vinyl stretched above to protect from rain. Goddamn stools – he knew he was too old to sit for long with his knees on either side of his bloody ears. But he'd chosen the disreputable spot for precisely these reasons. No one from his consular office would be caught dead in such a place. If this insane plan to steal the ruby didn't work out, he was indeed truly bollixed.

The teashop owner returned with a pint glass of sawdust-flecked ice and an open bottle. As he began to pour the beer over the ice, Geoffrey shot up his hand. "Stop. Set it on the bloody table. I don't want your plague-ridden ice." The man shrugged and skulked back to his place at the rear, mumbling under his breath.

Another man seated nearby laughed and sent a gob of crimson betel spit in Geoffrey's direction. "You one mean old bastard."

"You have no idea, my friend." Geoffrey dumped the ice and poured in tea from the steaming kettle. Swirling the weak liquid around in an attempt to sanitize the glass, he then emptied it on the ground and filled the glass with the urine-colored beer. He took a deep swallow. Taking out a new packet of Benson & Hedges, he removed the cellophane wrapper and flipped open the box, revealing the golden wrap within. With a shiver, he pulled out the foil tab. He didn't know why that moment gave him so much pleasure. Was it the sensation of the slight resistance, the fragrance of fresh cigarettes, or the anticipation of that first breath of smoke entering his body? He tugged a cigarette from its snug bed, flicked his lighter, and took a deep draw, loving the delicate crackle of igniting tobacco. As he expelled a plume of smoke from his nostrils, he frowned.

Raised in a typical upper-class British household, Geoffrey had followed his older brother to a prestigious public school where he had learned about much more than Chaucer. One afternoon, while wrestling in the cloakroom with a tow-headed boy named Stevie, he had discovered his true nature. A bit of buggery was expected in the boarding school setting, but Geoffrey took the offense to new heights. He had the bad manners to fall in love. It was the 1950s, and homosexuality was illegal in the UK, so the headmaster had called his parents, asking them to remove their disgraced son.

And now, here he was in Rangoon, disgraced yet again for loving the wrong person, exiled to this lowly diplomatic post. Fortunately, there were a few perks to make life livable. Squinting through cigarette smoke, he saw a young man striding toward him. He had a natural grace and a genuine smile, dressed in black trousers with a white shirt open at the collar. Something in Geoffrey's dry chest fluttered. "Well, hello, Maung Chit."

"Saya. You wait long time?"

"Only all my life."

"I no understand you talk." The boy dropped his friendly expression.

"I apologize. I've had a hard day. How are *you* today? Did you get the gift I left you last night?"

Maung Chit's smile returned, exposing the glowing white teeth Geoffrey loved. "Yes, you nice friend."

"I'm sure that man glaring at us over there would disagree." Geoffrey took a deep swallow of the weak beer.

Geoffrey had met Maung Chit by chance one morning in the consular office when the young man signed up for English classes. After a long, boozy lunch, they had come to an understanding that benefited them both.

"Is your cousin joining us today?"

"He still in village. Come soon."

Geoffrey restrained himself from tipping over the table. Meeting Maung Chit had been pleasant in many ways, but most noteworthy was his gossipy nature and the rumors he was willing to share with Geoffrey. It had been by complete chance that Maung Chit had mentioned his cousin's remarkable revelation about the Heart Stone. But time was running out.

He flicked his cigarette to the ground. "I hope so, dearie. Or I'll be in a lot of trouble. You don't want that, do you?"

A furrow appeared between the young man's ebony eyes. "Monsoon time, road very bad, he come soon."

This bloody medieval country. Geoffrey suppressed his frustration, not wanting to take it out on his friend. His gaze swallowed the young man's natural beauty, wondering how difficult it would be to escape together. A gilded apartment in Montparnasse, a villa in the Algarve, a teak hut in Bali – all filled with beauty, perhaps even love? Ha! An old man could dream, couldn't he? But he had to find the damned ruby, or there'd be no pretty home, no life at all. He was little more than a corpse already, future food for maggots and worms. He could almost feel Costa's breath down his neck.

Geoffrey's dark thoughts dispersed as a rainbow of three brightly dressed youths appeared, laughing and singing and calling out to Maung Chit. The first was a long-haired teen-ager with elaborately outlined eyes and a bright yellow sleeve-less shirt. The second had a purple Mohawk and sported a tight-fitting indigo tube top that revealed his soft belly. The third was older, elegant as a heron, with bright blue eyeshadow and a floral design tunic.

They grabbed seats and bunched around the tiny table like macarons in a box, ignoring the frowning proprietor.

"Ney kaung la, Maung Chit?"

"Ney kaung deh, Ko Myo," Maung Chit replied to the youth with the heavy eyeliner. "I very good." Turning to Geoffrey, he added, "These my special friends."

"I'm delighted to meet you all." Geoffrey signaled to the proprietor to bring more beer. He'd been dating the young Burmese for several months, but this was his first meeting with his friends. Geoffrey had yet to meet any other members of the reclusive Rangoon gay community. Burma was extremely conservative, and he'd been shocked to discover they still upheld the British colonial penal code outlawing sodomy.

"Would any of you like a cigarette?"

"Yes, please, Mister Sir," said purple Mohawk, accepting it with fingers covered with tiny cuts, some still healing.

"Goodness, what happened to your hands?"

The young man laughed. "No worry, sir. I work hair-dresser."

"Yes, he very good, very popular with movie star," Maung Chit said. "He cut your hair?"

"Oh, yes." Geoffrey ran his fingers through his thinning hair. "But only if you can make me handsome again." The group tittered, a sound as pleasant as songbirds.

"You plenty handsome, now," said the elegant one with the blue eyeshadow.

"This my friend, Aung Shwe. He powerful Nat Kadaw," Maung Chit said. "People not nice to some girlboy in Burma. But they scare of spirit-wife man. He make bad karma destiny."

Geoffrey had read about Burma's animistic worship dating from the pre-Buddhist era and the thirty-seven spirits called Nats, notorious troublemakers who had to be appeased with food and gifts. During special ceremonies, they were sometimes represented by transgender women and men who would dance themselves into altered states and offer predictions and advice to their followers. He loved the idea that such people could go into a trance and dispel karmic retribution to their haters. How ironic for a society that viewed homosexuality with ridicule and scorn.

"I'm honored to meet you."

"You must come to my next nat pwe celebration." His cornflower blue eyelids fluttered.

The proprietor set down a tray of bottles and glasses. "You pay, now," he demanded of the young men.

"All right, keep your knickers on." Geoffrey refused to allow an uneducated simpleton to ruin his magical moment with friends. The ruby's whereabouts would have to remain a mystery a bit longer.

Thierry would be furious.

CHAPTER ELEVEN

Mallory

The humid night set Mallory's prickly heat on an itchy rampage. Bored and naked, she lay under the air conditioning, familiar rage fermenting like sour soup, when the receptionist pushed a note under the door. Mr. Geoffrey had called to invite her for darts and dancing at the Australian Club. His driver waited outside. She yanked a dress over her head, excited to be doing something other than curse Martin. Drinking alone in the garden, watching the gardener skillfully hack each piece of grass by hand with his machete, had grown stale.

***

Edward carefully inched past parked cars along the narrow lane to drop her off. All the other drivers hung out near the compound gate smoking fiery seyboley cheroots that sputtered like roman candles. Their expressionless eyes followed her as she climbed out of the car and pulled her linen skirt free of her sweaty backside.

"Mallory?" The cute Australian military attaché from Sarkies Bar had also just arrived. "How are you?"

"I'm good, just looking for a cold beer. Have you seen Geoffrey? He promised me dancing tonight."

The Australian flashed crooked teeth. "I can help with the beer and the dancing, but I'm not sure about Geoffrey."

They stood in the doorway to a spacious room lined with bamboo paneling. A generator chugged nearby. Another power outage. Inside, two groups flung darts against tattered targets. The Australian grabbed a Fosters from a trough of ice brimming with the blue cans.

"Thank you." She rolled the cold can against her cheek. "This is exactly what I needed." Outside, through wide-open doors, Geoffrey waved his hands at her in a hurry-up gesture. "I owe you one," she smiled. The attaché's erect posture deflated as she waved goodbye.

"Well, hello, lovely lady." Geoffrey swiped air kisses in the region of her cheeks.

"Hello, yourself. What have you been up to today?"

"Usual mischief, I suppose."

Torches dotted the expansive lawn in a feeble attempt to push back the night. Flickering flames cast shadows across faces shiny with humidity. People complained that the brownouts were now more frequent and rife speculation blamed the situation on the corrupt government.

"There's someone I want you to meet." Geoffrey gently pushed her toward a fan palm at the far edge of the garden. "I think you will be marvelous friends."

A lanky man loomed in the half-light. With his back to the crowd and head tilted up, he seemed to be searching for something in the night sky. *When it's dark, look for stars*, her mother used to say. As they approached, he swiveled around, startling her with his quick, fluid movement.

"Thierry, here's the American I mentioned..."

Mallory peered up into the eyes of the most attractive man she had ever seen. Firelight from the torches only partially revealed his features, but glittering eyes and dark hair swept back from a high forehead were enough to create a warmth she felt in her belly.

"Bonsoir, mademoiselle." His voice was a perfect combination of honey and sand.

"Ah... hello."

"Well, well," Geoffrey chuckled. From the clubhouse, loud music suddenly blared, shifting their attention. INXS warned of *The Devil Inside*. "I think the time has come for some entertainment. Thierry, be a gentleman and ask the lady to dance."

In the end, she stayed very late, prickly heat discomfort forgotten as she took turns dancing, first with Thierry and then Geoffrey and then Thierry and then the Australian and then back to Thierry – fingers running down her spine, smokey lips brushing her ear. Crows were waking from their treetop nests when she arrived back at her hotel and stumbled into bed until the ring of the alarm.

"Bacon and fried eggs this morning," she told the waiter, in need of an American breakfast to overcome her hangover. With a careful sip of coffee so as not to move her pounding head too quickly, she noticed something peeking out from under the napkin. "What is this?"

"Fax letter for Miss," said the waiter as he carefully wrote down her order on his pad.

She slit open the envelope and gingerly removed the flimsy paper. "When did this arrive?"

"Yesterday time." The young man was eager to practice his English. "Miss out so now give."

Yesterday! Squinting at the smudged print, she wondered if the words were blurry or if she'd lost her sight. Martin and his investment group were coming to Rangoon in three days wanting her viability report, budget, and properties available for viewing.

Actually, only two days.

CHAPTER TWELVE

Zaw Wren

Colonel Zaw Wren of the de-commissioned Kachin Independence Army, sat at his desk with his chin in his hand and considered his fate. Luck had kept him alive on the battlefield for most of his life, but Luck turned her back on him when his leaders informed him of his new posting in the capital city of Rangoon. He found himself behind enemy lines, surrounded by the very people he'd fought for much of his life.

For decades, occupation by Britain and then Japan provided a shared adversary to the people of ethnically diverse Burma. Highland peoples, with their own languages and beliefs, ringed the central Burman-occupied Irrawaddy River valley. Joining forces, they fought together to expel the invaders.

With separation from the British Empire in 1948, a vacuum formed, quickly filled by the Burman majority. Armed insurgencies from the smaller states developed into full-fledged conflicts against the ruling military. Hatred of the dominant culture by the marginalized groups of the periphery, including the Kachin, led to Burma's dubious honor of having the longest-running civil war in modern history. Now, after many false starts, a historic ceasefire agreement was signed between the government and the Kachin Independence Organization.

The loyal Colonel with a cool head and excellent language skills was chosen to act as the liaison to his former enemies. Zaw sighed at the enormity of the task before him. At least the fighting had stopped. His mission was diplomatic, but he was unhappy knowing he would always be considered an enemy and an outsider. Lonely in the capital city, he wondered if a stain of hatred coated his features and kept people away.

Shoving a stack of fluttering papers to the edge of his desk, he sighed again. The untrustworthy ministers might take months just to agree on what type of paper to use in the agreement, let alone what it would say. It was a miracle the ceasefire was actually finalized. It was lunchtime, and he started gathering his notes. As he reached for the door, it swung open, and a slim, young man wearing a bright blue longyi stood in the entry.

"Colonel Zaw Wren, I assume?" The man smiled brightly and held out his hand in the Western manner.

"Yes?"

"I am Ko Kyaw!" said the fellow, as if stating the obvious. "I have come to befriend you, our dear Kachin cousin, and welcome you to the delights of beautiful Rangoon in exchange for learning about you people of the north. I have never been farther than Mandalay myself and take great interest in the varied cultures of our land. Please allow me to be your guide to this wonderful city."

Taking the offered hand and looking into the young man's clear eyes, Zaw was relieved to finally identify the military intelligence agent he'd been expecting. He knew that a former enemy, regardless of current standing as an advisor, would be closely watched by the paranoid, xenophobic leaders. The usual spies used by General Khin Nyunt, head of MI, were anything but subtle with their aviator-style sunglasses and arrogant attitude. But this callow boy seemed an inexperienced operative. If he was indeed what he appeared, then Colonel Zaw Wren wasn't considered important enough to send someone more brutal. A weight lifted from his chest.

"I would be most honored for you to be my guide. Shall we begin with a beer and some lunch?"

"Oh no," said Ko Kyaw. "I am Buddhist and follow the many precepts of our Lord Buddha, including the prohibition against alcohol."

"It would be my honor to have you be my guest."

"Well, I do so want to make you welcome... Perhaps I can relax the rules just once. After all, the Lord Buddha also teaches moderation in all things."

"Thank you," Zaw smiled wryly.

They headed out the door of Zaw's office and down the corridor to the crumbling marble stairway. The Ministry of Defense was a socialist-dreary, multi-storied building on Signal Pagoda Road with many uses in its long life. Rumors said the minister had recently sold the property to a developer to build a new hotel. The spot where people spat their red-tinged betel in the corner of the battered stairwell resembled the site of a massacre. The brass spittoons of the old days had been stolen long ago. Ko Kyaw continued his meaningless chatter as Zaw remembered enough bloody battlefields for one lifetime. They descended to the busy street below and strolled across the bridge over the railroad tracks.

***

Seated on plastic stools at his preferred sidewalk tea shop, Zaw nodded hello to the woman stationed behind the makeshift counter. Her few strands of dyed black hair were pulled tightly into a bun; her red and yellow striped longyi wrapped up and around her massive belly. Though not a beauty, she made the most delicious fried mutton and potato samosas in town. She also gave Zaw a fair price on his favorite Mandalay-brand beer.

"Ice today, Bomugyi?" she called to Zaw.

"Yes, two bottles and a plate of freshest samosas."

"She knows you are a Colonel?" Ko Kyaw raised his eyebrows.

"She knows everything," laughed Zaw. "These street vendors miss nothing." Across the road, Bogyoke Market bustled with shoppers. Zaw liked to observe people. As a ghost in a foreign city, the company of strangers was now his life.

Ko Kyaw downed half a glass of beer in one draught. "Oh my, this will go to my head," he giggled. "Thank you for your kind invitation. Please tell me, how do you find our fair capital?"

Zaw shrugged noncommittally as he plucked a crispy samosa and dropped it into his mouth. With a swallow, he said, "I like the food."

"Yes, yes," the young man nodded vigorously. "These tasty snacks are Indian, of course. My mother makes even better." He wiped a dribble of grease from his chin with a handkerchief. "When did you arrive, and where do you stay?"

"I've been here almost three weeks," Zaw said. "I sleep in the dormitory for single men at the Judson Baptist church, though I pass most of the time at my desk. Do you work at the War Office?" Zaw knew he wouldn't get a truthful reply, but he enjoyed the banter.

"Yes, I work as secretary to Colonel Tin Tut, right down the corridor."

Zaw raised his hand for another bottle of beer. "Is he associated with the peace accord?" He'd met the Burmese colonel when he arrived but had never seen him with any staff.

"Not directly," Ko Kyaw prevaricated. "Enough work chat. Please tell me about your home. Are you originally from Myitkyina? Do you own a sword? Do you have many brothers and sisters? What is your father's name?" His questions tumbled out in a torrent.

Zaw understood this unsophisticated questioning concerned details the Burmese would already have on file. And the second bottle of beer had definitely relaxed his defenses.

He was beginning to like the young man. "Of course, I have a traditional sword. Kachin people are warriors. My father's village is in the northernmost part of the country, at the edge of the eastern Himalayan Mountains. I returned only once as a man."

"Why is that." Ko Kyaw snatched the last samosa with a young boy's grin. "Don't you miss your family?"

"Why do you think?" Zaw regarded the young spy with cold eyes.

"Oh, yes, of course," Ko Kyaw stumbled over words. "The conflict in the north has lasted many decades."

Zaw never regretted his decision to follow his father into the insurgency. His people were ferocious fighters, and enemies were plentiful. Sovereignty was a worthy cause, and he would never relent, even when posted within the viper's nest. Yet sometimes, in rare moments, he allowed himself to drift into a favorite daydream of simple days passed along icy rivers fed by ancient glaciers. Fishing for his dinner while searching for the rubies that tumbled down from above, bits of fire to be captured from the earth's stony heart. A wife to cook the fish and warm his bed. A son to love and teach life's lessons.

He shook himself to the present. Colonel Zaw Wren was a soldier; it was the only way of life he knew. The vision of his homeland was only that: a dream, a weakness he sometimes allowed himself for a few brief moments before sleep. Even his father had not traveled home after the Americans recruited him to fight against the Japanese during World War II. Zaw Wren had only returned once – to bury his father's bones.

"What are you doing here, Ko Kyaw?" Zaw asked. "Shouldn't a handsome young man like you choose another path? What does your mother think?"

Ko Kyaw emptied his glass and returned Zaw's gaze with a resolute look. "I am where I'm supposed to be, Colonel. I pray to Lord Buddha that this fighting will end one day."

"Amen to that." Zaw drained his glass. "Another bottle?"

"If you insist, my dear friend!" Ko Kyaw's simpering persona reappeared. "And another plate of samosas?"

The sun blazed down on the crowded street as the noon hour passed. The men lapsed into a companionable silence satiated by fried food and beer. Across the boulevard, a Western couple emerged from the shadow of the market entrance and stood blinking in the sunlight. Zaw discerned an unusual tension between the man and woman. In his limited experience, foreigners could afford to be easy and happy.

"Oh my," exclaimed Ko Kyaw. "They're from *Breakfast At Tiffany's!*"

"Breakfast At Tiffany's?"

"Oh, yes! My most favorite film! Audrey Hepburn and George Peppard, the very best romantic comedy of all time," he gushed. "These people, just there, look exactly like those marvelous actors themselves, in the flesh!"

The attractive couple stood unspeaking, their bodies tense. Had they been fighting? Street vendors squatting along the sidewalk selling seyboley cheroots and roasted corn on the cob called out to them, but they didn't respond. A black-market money changer approached, and the foreign man gave him such a thunderous expression that the tout stopped dead in his tracks. A car pulled up, and the woman yanked open the door, throwing herself into the backseat. The European man slammed her door shut instead of following her into the car. A scowl marred the tall man's handsome face as he raised his hand to summon a second taxi. There was something familiar about him that made Zaw uneasy. He recognized a propensity for violence when he saw it.

Colonel Zaw Wren of the Kachin Independence Army slowly poured another glass of beer, wondering at the beauty of the Western woman, and why she accompanied a man with a killer's eyes.

CHAPTER THIRTEEN

Thierry

Thierry restrained himself from throwing the telephone against the wall. Two hours wasted attempting to reach his gem broker contacts, to the chagrin of the front desk clerk who had to place each call through the antiquated phone system. The rainy season wreaked havoc on the dysfunctional telephone lines of the city; it was a miracle he'd been able to connect with even three of the seven names on his list.

"No sir, sorry sir, that number not working." The young clerk was the same one who had served him breakfast. Did he sleep under the reception counter?

Contacting these men by telephone might put them at risk with the authorities. Who knows who might be listening? But he had no choice. How could there not be rumors circulating the country about the ancient ruby if it had indeed reappeared? What a triumph for the Burmese government to bring the heart of Burma home after almost a millennium. But the generals might not know. Could a private individual retain such a secret? Geoffrey couldn't be the only one with information.

"Try again," he said.

He stretched out on the white cotton bedcover, his body longer than the bed, hands behind his head. The pillows were pitiful and the bed hard; he missed his comfortable feather-down bed. Paris seemed like another world, far away. He wondered about the conditions of the place where his father was being held – if Roger was still alive.

"Number no good." The clerk was getting testy.

He would go mad if he didn't leave the room. He needed some distraction. "Fine, we stop for now."

Picking up his pack of Marlboros, the corner of a business card peeked out. The American woman had stood out from the pitiful gathering of remote island castaways. After dancing for hours, she'd written her name on the back of her hotel's business card.

"Actually, there is one more number to try."

***

The vast white-tiled room of the Imperial Garden resembled a subway station in a bad suburb of Paris. The only green to be seen were random pots of bamboo surrounding a smiling, fat Buddha. An unctuous Chinese man in black trousers and a white shirt greeted him at the door and then whisked him to a table large enough to serve ten. The air conditioning was so high Thierry imagined he could see his breath. Families of two or three generations crowded smaller tables – apparently, the waiter wanted to keep the foreigner far away in the Siberian end of the room.

Out the plate-glass window, a dilapidated teak house – its original grandeur evident in the graceful carvings adorning the eves – leaned over the side of the muddy street. Directly adjacent, in stark contrast, lurked a concrete bunker of a house with heavy iron bars on all the windows.

He sensed rather than saw the American woman enter the restaurant. Noisy babble subsided as the customers observed the beautiful foreigner shake rain from her hair. The host almost fell rushing to greet her and then led her to Thierry's table.

"I must look a mess. I think I need a towel." Mallory plucked at her blouse.

"Bonjour." As he kissed her cheeks, he inhaled a light rose fragrance with a hint of something musky. He wished he had done a better job shaving. "I had a marvelous evening last night. I didn't know if you would be recovered enough for brunch. But I had to leave my closet of a room for some fresh air, so I took a chance."

"I'm glad you did. I had literally just received a fax from my boss, who is arriving the day after tomorrow. A distraction is exactly what I need, so I don't chew my own arm off." She looked down at her gnawed fingertips. "Dim sum with you sounded much more appealing than soggy bacon."

The waiter deposited a pot of fragrant jasmine tea and pointed to the tray that held cups, chopsticks, and glass jars of dubious condiments.

"Do you like Chinese dumplings? This restaurant is supposedly famous for them."

An elderly woman, her grin missing several teeth, pushed a steaming trolley up to their table. "Madam, like?" The woman pointed to multiple round bamboo baskets. Like performing a magician's trick, she whisked the covers off one after the other, revealing various dumplings. "*Shiu mai, har gau? Char siu bao?* Very delicious," she cackled.

"Two of each," Thierry said. "Does the American chef approve?"

"Oh, yes – but extra pot stickers!"

Soon, tiny dishes covered the table. Thierry regarded the condiments with suspicion. "Which do you recommend?"

Mallory picked up one of the jars filled with a vivid red sauce. "I like most of them. Hoisin adds sweet, soy sauce for salt, and chili oil for heat. How do you like your flavors?"

"Salty and sweet," he grinned, imagining what her lips would be like to kiss.

Mallory spooned a bit from each of the jars. "Well, here you go, monsieur, bon appétit."

Thierry picked up the plastic chopsticks and twirled one around his fingers like a drummer from a heavy metal band. "Like this?" He skillfully plucked a dumpling, dipped the bite into chili oil, and then plopped it into his mouth.

"Okay, show off," Mallory laughed.

As they ate, Thierry noticed Mallory's joking didn't reach her eyes. The previous evening, there had been little talking, only dancing and drinking, so this morning, he listened closely as she explained her work in Rangoon. He found her more mature than his initial impression, and wondered why she carried the weight of such sadness. She resembled a feral cat someone had discarded.

"Mallory, your eyes are an unusual color. Like green tourmaline or even a dark emerald. Do they change with your moods?" As he leaned forward, he noticed her necklace was the same one she'd worn the previous evening.

"No one ever told me if they do," she said.

Thierry leaned even closer. Red glass nestled in a Celtic knot setting dangled from a tarnished silver chain. "And what is the story of your pendant?"

"It belonged to my mother."

Thierry refrained from rolling his eyes at the tawdry jewelry. Why did women wear such garbage?

A furrow appeared on Mallory's forehead. "I know it's not worth much, but she died when I was young, and I keep it as a good luck charm – though it didn't bring either of us much luck." Her laugh fell flat.

Thierry could see it was old and made of cheap sterling silver; some of the prongs holding the stone were damaged. From nowhere, Janice and her glittering sapphire necklace came to mind. Another American woman, but older and wealthier, her overly taut neck and Botox-frozen face a testimonial to her need to remain young at any cost. Looking at the cheap pendant hanging around Mallory's smooth neck, he imagined the Heart Stone. He wouldn't need any woman, rich or otherwise, with that in his possession. But in the meantime, the American was a lovely amusement. He sipped his tea, pondering a brilliant idea. How to both seduce the woman *and* reach an important contact.

"Have you been to Scott Market yet?" he asked, balancing a final dumpling with his chopsticks. "Talented craftsmen could remake your necklace for a reasonable price. Perhaps even replace the glass with a real ruby."

"Maybe." She pushed away her empty plate. "But I think I'll just keep it as is. Now it's your turn. Last night you mentioned that your business here is purchasing gemstones. How does one become an expert?"

"Like anything, with study and passion." He signaled for the check, not wanting to delve too deeply into his purpose for being in Rangoon. "Let's finish up, and I'll introduce you to Daw Khin Myint. She might do a better job of convincing you to buy a real ruby."

***

Bogyoke Aung San Market, formerly Scott Market during British times, was popular with locals and tourists alike. Anything was for sale – from antique puppets and ornate lacquerware to flip flops. Cobblestone alleyways bordered the massive art deco building on both sides. A labyrinth of inner aisles had once trapped Thierry for over an hour. An open-sided tin roof soared overhead with dark wooden rafters. Beggars, Buddhist nuns offering prayers for a few kyats, and young girls selling sandalwood-scented fans jostled visitors while merchants called out greetings from their small stalls. Shops lined the central walkway where gem traders displayed colorful jewelry of every variety imaginable. Some were fake, but most were real.

"How can all this wealth be out in the open like this?" Mallory remarked, strolling down the center of the market.

"Won't someone steal it?"

"You forget where we are. Burma is a repressive police state with the greatest surveillance system in the world – informants and fear." Steering her by the elbow, he directed her to a tiny shop off the main thoroughfare. Unlike the other stalls displaying gems of many colors, this had only rubies.

"Mingalaba," said the smiling middle-aged woman seated behind the glass case. She wore a colorful yellow eingyi blouse that matched the blossom tucked into her hair.

"Mallory, this is Daw Khin Myint. She is a business colleague whom I met during a previous visit."

"You have returned?" the shopkeeper asked Thierry.

"Yes, you have the best rubies in Rangoon. I wish to show some to my friend, Miss Jones." He leaned forward and lowered his voice. "Also, to inquire if you've heard of anything unusual appearing after a long absence?"

The woman's eyes swiveled to the right and the left. "No, nothing out of the ordinary, Monsieur Aubert."

Thierry hid his disappointment. Of course, she wouldn't tell him anything in front of a stranger, even if she had heard something. He would have to speak with her privately.

Daw Khin Myint said, "May I offer you a cold drink, Miss? I'm sorry our country is quite warm..."

"I'm getting accustomed to the heat," Mallory said. "It's the humidity that gets to me. But something cold sounds nice."

A young girl appeared with two tall, narrow stools for them to sit on, then scurried off to fetch bottles of soda. The shopkeeper pulled out a tray from below the counter. The colors ranged from a delicate pink blush to dried black blood.

"Are these all rubies?" Mallory said. "I've never seen colors like this. It's like they're alive. I can't believe these were once rocks under the ground."

He brought his attention back. "Yes, these are all created, or, one might say, baked over eons in the belly of the earth. But, like the excellent recipe, the mineral corundum 'spice' must be of the perfect measurement. A bit more heat or less geological damage, and we see the varied results before us."

"What an unusual color." Mallory nudged a tear-shaped gem with her fingertip. "Is it purple or red? It keeps shifting."

"You have a discerning eye," Daw Khin Myint said. "This is from our most famous ruby mine – Mogok, to the north."

Thierry set the gem on his palm. "Have you heard of pigeon blood rubies?"

"It makes them more valuable, right?"

"Yes, much more. But the value is not just the color; it's also the fluorescence, the unique glow. Daw Khin Myint, may I have your loupe?" Holding the stone up to a nearby desk lamp, Thierry peered at the ruby between his fingertips. "Regardez, Mallory, you will be pleased."

She leaned against Thierry for a better view. "What am I looking for?"

"Rutile. The tiny spider web of silk which brings light to the dark heart of the ruby." He put the tiny teardrop in her palm. "Shall we compare this to your necklace? We can exchange the glass for something real."

Mallory's head jerked up, her emerald eyes black. "No thanks. I'll pass."

"But, don't you want to at least have it reset?" He couldn't imagine why she would want to keep such trash against her skin.

"No." Her tone was final.

"As you wish," he said. "But you must have this one. Some jewels carry a certain vibration, and this particular jewel spoke to you for a reason."

He nodded to Daw Khin Myint, who polished the stone then slipped it into a velvet pouch. All women loved the gift of jewels. Thierry placed the bag into Mallory's hands and bent to kiss her. He was astonished when she pushed him away.

"Thank you, Daw Khin Myint," Mallory said. "I hope to come back sometime and shop on my own." She turned and marched away without a glance at Thierry.

Thierry shrugged and returned the ruby to the Burmese gem merchant. He rushed to catch up as Mallory strode through the market. At the entrance, she put her hand in the air to call the attention of her driver, then finally turned to him. "Thanks for brunch, Thierry. And the lesson about rubies. But I've got a ton of work to do before my boss comes." She squinted against the bright sun. "Can you get a taxi back to your hotel?"

"Of course," Thierry said, disappointed they wouldn't spend the rest of the day tossing in his narrow bed. "Shall we meet later at Sarkies?"

"Unlikely. I'm going to be super busy."

When her car and driver pulled up, she got in without another word. Thierry wasn't accustomed to women brushing him off like a whining mosquito. He slammed the car door shut behind her and turned away without a backward glance. He purposely didn't watch as they pulled away into traffic.

Suddenly, he felt ashamed of his behavior, acting like a foolish boy. He had a job to do and there wasn't time for such games. If he weren't careful, his father would be dead, and he might spend the rest of his days in prison. As he raised his hand to hail a taxi, he locked eyes with a soldier sitting at a street cafe on the other side of the road.

The man wore an unfamiliar dark green uniform, and his deep-set eyes glowered at Thierry from across the boulevard.

CHAPTER FOURTEEN

Mallory

The electricity died again, and silence woke Mallory from a troubled sleep. The hotel's generator usually kicked right on, so the power outages weren't notable. But now, it felt like it had been off for a long while. Brick-like humidity pressed on her chest. As she sat up, the pounding dream returned.

She'd been in a terrible storm on a pitching boat. In the darkness, a lantern swung on the mast ahead. Crawling on her belly across the slippery deck she found not a light, but the pale face of her former roommate. Liz's mouth worked as if shouting, but no sound came out. In the dream, Mallory pulled herself up the side of the vessel and stared down into an ocean of churning grief.

Someone tapped on her hotel door. "Miss?"

Her battery-operated travel clock blinked 4:16 a.m. as wisps of the nightmare dispersed. She fumbled to the door after unsuccessfully flicking the light switch. "What's happening?"

The attendant was an older man she'd met only once before. He held an old-fashioned oil lamp aloft, and, for a moment, the dream still swirled around her. "There was an earthquake, Miss. I check the guests."

"An earthquake?"

"Yes, it is quite common in Burma. Electric come soon. Please take this." He handed her the lamp. "I bring you a cup of Horlicks?"

"No, thank you."

With a nod, the man slipped away into the shadow, his white shirt disappearing like a ghost. The lamp created a cozy atmosphere, but the heat steadily mounted. She hoped the electricity would roar back soon, or she'd have to risk mosquitos in the garden. She shot a brutal glance toward her trusty guidebook. It didn't mention earthquakes.

Mallory mulled Thierry's comment about some rubies containing unique energy. Her home in the Pacific Northwest was known for its natural disaster potential: volcanoes, tsunamis, and earthquakes. Most people went about their everyday lives, oblivious to the earth's power lurking in wait just beneath their feet. Just ask the fifty-two people who were asphyxiated in May 1980 when Mount Saint Helens blew her top. Mallory clearly remembered the drifts of volcanic ash – like grains of glassy sand – that had scoured every surface of her small town for weeks.

What if that pent-up intensity could enter the groundwater or food chain? Little furious molecules of energy infusing every bite of food or sip of water. Manny, Mallory's father, had undoubtedly been a direct channel to some hard-core geothermal-level anger, taking it out on her mother Rachel's face and body with magma-like fury.

One evening, like any other, he'd been practicing his favorite game of throwing cans of Rainier Beer at her mother. As Rachel sobbed, curled on her side next to the television set, Mallory climbed up the back of the sofa and grabbed her daddy's wrist as he pulled back to toss another can. She chomped down as hard as a six-year-old could manage, causing her front teeth – one of which was already loose – to stay lodged in the back of his hand as he howled with pain and jumped up. With a swipe, Manny backhanded her against the wall, where she fell, stunned, and pressed her hands over her ears, muffling the horrible whine her mommy made as her daddy kicked her belly.

Don't make him angry, Rachel had whispered through split lips as she put Mallory to bed that night. *Always be a good girl.*

Later, after Mallory had discovered the camaraderie of a commercial kitchen, she wondered why she and her mother hadn't formed an alliance against the man's violence. But they hadn't. And besides, what could a little girl have done? She would have to wait a few more years to learn how.

Electric power or not, Martin was coming tomorrow, and she had to be ready. Rolling off the bed, she tugged out the suitcase that served as her office and began to review her notes by the lamp's light. An hour later, the AC surged on. Giving thanks to Benjamin Franklin, she spread-eagled on the cotton spread, savoring the cool waterfall of a breeze. A velvet moth threw itself against the ceiling light and drew her attention to an enormous crack marring the stucco of the wall. Worried the building was falling, she scrambled off the bed and rushed to the dining room, wearing only her tee shirt and panties. The sleepy waiter wasn't in the least concerned as he snuck peeks at her bare legs and pointed out other whitewashed cracks from previous quakes. Fantastic – just like home.

Small gardenias spewed their heavy, old lady's perfume as she waited for breakfast in the garden. Better to be outside in case of aftershocks. The tireless gardener squatted a few yards away, cheroot in the corner of his mouth as he made his way across the grass, cutting one blade at a time. Her spiral note-book fluttered in the sudden breeze as she tore out pages of notes, adding them to the presentation folder containing her contract and fax communications from Martin. One more day. Waiting. Waiting. Ready as she would ever be.

"Guest, Miss!" called the desk clerk, trotting to keep in front of a man striding across the lawn with a stocky build and heavy bald head. His linen suit appeared expensive but without the attractive rumpled effect, Geoffrey managed so effortlessly. Black hair sprouted from the 'v' of his unbuttoned shirt, and a flashy Rolex winked from his cuff.

"Mallory Jones, I presume?" The man chuckled as if he'd told a funny joke and held out his hand. "It's nice to meet you finally. I'm Martin Payne."

Mallory jumped up to take the outstretched palm, confused by the disconnect between the familiar voice and gangster-looking man. "Martin. I expected you tomorrow." She moderated the sharpness in her voice. "Did I misunderstand?"

"Yes, well, I came a bit early and for a bit of a look-see around."

"You came early? From Hong Kong?" There was only one plane a day arriving from Hong Kong, and it was in the evening, so he'd been here at least a day. She noticed a taxi parked under a tree, the driver leaning against the reception door, chatting to the receptionist as he waited. They had slipped in when she wasn't paying attention.

"Let's have a seat, shall we?" Martin shrugged off his suit to reveal a shirt almost transparent with damp perspiration.

Mallory didn't know whether to be happy or concerned by his unexpected appearance. "We can go inside if you prefer, where it's cooler."

"Actually, I'm on the way to the airport and in a small rush."

Mallory fell back into her seat. "I don't understand."

The server crept toward them. "You want cold drink? Coffee?"

Martin glanced around as if he might find a well-stocked bar nearby. "Do you have any *good* whiskey?" His imperial tone implied disdain for whatever the Burmese man might offer. "It's after five somewhere in the world." He laughed again, amused by his own cleverness.

"Johnny Walker Red, sir." The young man was almost trembling.

"Well, all right. Bring me a whiskey soda with ice. But be sure it's clean ice. I don't want to get sick, ha-ha." He turned to Mallory. "What will you have?" as if he was the host and she the guest.

"Just coffee, please." She smiled at the young waiter to make up for Martin's rudeness while calculating if she could fit her hands around his fat neck.

Martin cleared his throat as if preparing for a speech. "The group is grateful for everything you've accomplished thus far. Excellent work." He checked his gold watch. "Coming all this way, and such."

"But you don't know what I've done." She picked up her presentation and held it out to him.

Ignoring the folder, he continued, "I know we agreed to a feasibility study and you possibly staying on and running the restaurant, but based on our findings, we've decided to nix the project. Our local sources tell us it's too early for a project like ours."

Mallory placed the folder on the table as if it was a bomb. "Local sources?"

Just then, the server returned, balancing a tray with their drinks. Martin grabbed his glass and gulped it down, the ice rattling and making damp spots on his trousers. "Bring another," he demanded. "Yes, we have a contact at the Ministry of Hotels and Tourism, and he says it's just too soon for something private. A joint venture is the way to go, and my little group is too small for that."

"And you didn't learn this *before* hiring me?"

Martin squinted like she'd farted or something else terribly rude. "We'll let you keep whatever remains of the five thousand and, of course, give you a tidy fee for your time and effort." He twisted around to pull an envelope from his inside jacket pocket and placed it on the folder. "This should take the sting out, I reckon."

"Take the sting out?" Mallory spat. Her temper rose up the

back of her throat, burning like lava from the earth's center. "You'll be lucky if I don't sue your ass." About to explode, she jumped up, her chair toppling sideways.

Martin's placid face shifted, and granite replaced the bumbling good old boy charade. "Best of luck with that, Mallory. Just take the bloody money." As she glared, not knowing what to say, he tugged on his jacket and strode back to the waiting taxi.

The server rushed out with Martin's second drink. Mal grabbed it and hurled it at the British man's back. The golden fluid arced through the air as the glass thudded on the lawn a few feet from the driveway. Martin only shook his massive head and got into the car. She needed a weapon. The gardener's machete leaned against a nearby tree. She hefted the tool, assessing the comforting weight as if she might use it in her kitchen, and trotted after the taxi as it rolled down the driveway.

Mal remembered a big-bosomed lady, smelling of gardenia talc and Jesus, who had wanted to take in the poor little motherless child, no older than seven. But Mallory missed her own mother, and one day, she'd shoved the woman to the ground, kicking her where she fell. But her dead mother's voice had whispered, *No, bad girl!* and the rage was tamped down, shoved into a secret room, the door locked. No one wanted a bad child.

At the end of the driveway, Mal stopped. The full moon of Martin's face receded out of sight in the taxi's back window. He got away. Anger boiling, she thrust the blade into the earth.

At that moment, a Range Rover pulled up. The window rolled down, and Geoffrey peered out. "What are you doing out here on the street, my sweet?" He checked the rearview mirror with a frown. "And who are you chasing with that machete? I've come to take you to breakfast at the club."

With practiced ease, Mallory swallowed her fury. "Okay, Geoffrey. That sounds terrific."

CHAPTER FIFTEEN

Geoffrey

Geoffrey sat in his usual corner at Madame Laurent's next to the overgrown philodendron, sipping a tepid flute of Moldovan champagne as Piaf howled bloody *La Vie En Rose* on the record player. The only other guests were a pair of middle-aged men from the Italian embassy. Thierry was late.

In those first horrible months after arriving in Rangoon, two things kept Geoffrey sane: history books from the British Consulate library and Madame Yvette Laurent. Transition from his diplomatic posting in the City of Lights to the City of Relentless Heat and Impossible Smells was soul-crushing and Geoffrey took his exile hard. With no one in whom to confide, he was slowly going mad.

Yvette Laurent and her establishment had changed everything. Rumors abounded, but no one knew the true story of how the Frenchwoman came to own an upscale brothel for diplomats and wealthy businessmen in the best part of the city. Always discrete, Madame offered cheap champagne and watered-down cocktails along with young girls and the occasional boy.

The two unlikely friends discovered a shared appreciation for French baroque furniture and libertine young men. No longer young and slim but still painfully blonde, Madame exhibited a sly appeal many found attractive. Clicking about on the wooden floor in her kitten-heeled mules, she wore tailored Thai silk dresses in bright colors which emphasized her considerable bosom. Geoffrey passed many evenings tucked into the corner of Madame's bar, getting pleasantly drunk and reliving better days. At the end of the night, she would join him, kicking off her heels and singing in her booming off-key alto to music from the record player. Madame owned only three albums, two of which were Edith Piaf.

That night he'd drunk himself into a state fearing he might explode with excitement. The cousin of his boyfriend, Maung Chit, had finally revealed the surprising location of the ruby. A monastery was the last place he expected the ruby to be hiding. What would monks want with something so valuable? Then again, he thought, the bloody country was chockablock with gold-plated pagodas dangling precious jewels from the rafters like bonbons.

Thierry could open a safe as easily as a woman's blouse, so grabbing the stone from a group of sheet-draped do-gooders should be a snap. As far as Geoffrey knew, security in all those monasteries and pagodas was non-existent. No Burmese would risk burning in Buddhist hell for an eternity of lifetimes. They might actually pull off this crazy feat. But he trusted the Frenchman as much as a cobra in a hen house.

Speak of the devil, and he appeared. Thierry towered in the doorway, his dark eyes glowering. Geoffrey signaled for another bottle. "Bonsoir, mon ami. You found Madame's establishment without difficulty?"

Thierry lowered himself into the chair. "Yes, the taxi driver knew the place. Is there news?"

Careful, careful, Geoffrey chided himself. He really shouldn't have drunk so much. "I'm delighted to say there is news."

"And...?" Thierry lit a cigarette and exhaled smoke from his nostrils in a heavy stream.

Hysteria tickled Geoffrey's throat -Thierry looked exactly

like a dragon. A giggle escaped. He washed it back with a slug of wine. "Not so fast, my friend; we don't want to run off half-cocked." Thierry's mouth pursed in disgust at the mention of cocks, which only fueled Geoffrey's laughter. "We must craft our approach with the utmost care," he choked, riding a drunken wave of mirth.

"No, *my friend*, you just tell me where it is." Thierry's voice rose above a whisper, and the Italians looked their way.

Geoffrey made a shushing sound and scraped his chair closer. "The boy confirmed the location. It's in a monastery east of Mandalay."

"A monastery? Well, that makes it easy, right?" Thierry's voice rasped near Geoffrey's ear, smoke and champagne on his breath. "What's the name of the place? Is there a safe?"

"I'll hold on to that information for now," Geoffrey said. "Let's plan our strategy."

Thierry laughed. "What *strategy*? You tell me where it is, and I take it."

"I'm going north with you. Together, we find it and bring it back to Rangoon." His sweaty palms left smears on his wine glass.

Thierry stared at him with such a look Geoffrey feared he might piss himself. "You would be in the way, old man," he hissed.

Madame Laurent made her entrance with a swish of silk and a cloud of perfume. Acknowledging her other customers, she headed to their table in the corner. "My darling Geoffrey, who have you brought me? Are you new to our little island, mon cher?" She bent over to give Thierry air kisses and an unimpeded view of her cleavage.

Grateful for the distraction, Geoffrey introduced Thierry and stood to pull out a seat for Madame. "Please join us, my dear."

"Merci, but only for a moment." As she sat, the waiter rushed over with her usual glass of Ricard and a tiny water pitcher. He poured a splash into the golden pastis, and the drink turned cloudy. "What can I bring you this evening?" she said. "Another bottle of champagne, some delicate company, perhaps, hmm?"

"We're fine with the wine. Wherever did you find a Moldovan vintage the heat hasn't ruined?" Geoffrey said.

"Oh, I have my ways." She fluttered her heavily-mascaraed eyes at Thierry. "What brings a handsome compatriot to this place?"

"Do you mean Burmanie or this bordel?" Thierry crossed his slender legs and blew a plume of smoke at Madame's powdered face.

Geoffrey sputtered. "Thierry, no need to be like that. Madame is an extremely important friend."

Madame tapped her pink-tipped nails on the marble tabletop and then reached over to flick a bit of tobacco from Thierry's lip. "Naughty boys are so delightful, don't you think, Geoffrey? Especially the beautiful ones." She rose from the chair and adjusted her bra strap. "Call me if you need anything, mon cher. The nights here can be lonely." She looked at Geoffrey. "And you, my friend, be careful of new friends."

As she rose to greet a cluster of Russians coming in the door, Geoffrey restrained himself from kicking Thierry in the shin. "What are you thinking? She might be useful to us later."

"She's a cow, and I hate women like her."

"Ha! That's rich coming from you. Don't forget how we met. I'm familiar with your preference for so-called cows. Did this little project make you forget your true expertise?" Thierry's face cringed. He really wasn't all that handsome.

"You're a fool," Thierry said. "As soon as I know the exact location, I won't need you anymore. Do you understand?"

"Exactly why we will be inseparable. I have too much to lose to allow you to go roaming around on your own." Geoffrey jabbed his finger into Thierry's chest. "You need my access to the British diplomatic pouch to get the gem out of the country. Nothing in that bag passes through customs." He leaned back. "As we planned – you steal, and I smuggle."

"So, you think we just become invisible as we travel to this mysterious monastery? No one watching us in this Orwellian country of secret watchers and spies? I'm just a tourist. But you? A British diplomat. You will be under surveillance outside of the capital, non?"

Geoffrey thought for a moment. Thierry made a good point. All diplomats had to inform the Home Ministry of the purpose of any travel when they moved about the country. His dark red diplomatic passport would be eye-catching for any suspicious hotel clerk.

"What if I pose as a tourist," he said. "Traveling with my American niece and her French boyfriend on a scenic weekend getaway?" He grinned at his own cleverness.

"If you're thinking of Mallory, why would we tell her our plan?"

"We won't, of course," Geoffrey recalled the sight of Mallory standing in the road gripping a machete, looking like Joan of Arc about to head into battle. "Actually, she might be more useful than we think. We just invite her for the weekend – she won't have a clue about the real purpose of the trip. After we're successful, we abandon her upcountry and hotfoot it back." Geoffrey didn't linger on what *abandon* might mean for the young woman. She was lovely but he couldn't risk her becoming a problem. "As we already discussed," he pushed his face close to Thierry's. "I'll put *it* in a special confidential envelope to be delivered to the UK via the pouch. I leave Rangoon on a sudden family emergency, go back home, and retrieve my envelope at the home office in London. We meet there to hand it over to Costa and collect our earnings. Perfect plan."

Geoffrey quivered in his seat. It was all coming together and he would finally be free of that gangster Maurice Costa. He'd already started the process to procure a passport for his boyfriend. With the proceeds from the sale of the ruby, they could disappear into the proverbial sunset. He turned his face to hide his brimming eyes.

Thierry leaned forward. "I will never allow the Heart Stone out of my sight. Bringing the American woman is not a terrible idea, but the stone stays with me. I have a better plan to smuggle it out." He drained his glass. "And *you* will have to manage Mallory."

"We'll see about that." Geoffrey's voice rose as the hysteria returned. "For now, we're joined at the hip until this is bloody well finished." He crashed the empty bottle into the silver bucket. "Another bottle," he shouted to the barman across the room.

The other guests looked and then turned away at the sight of yet another drunken Englishman. He better succeed, or he was a dead man.

CHAPTER SIXTEEN

Mallory

The explanation wasn't going well. Across the table, Cho Cho regarded her with an anxious expression. "So, you are *not* opening a restaurant?"

"No." Mallory struggled to keep her frustration in check as she explained again. "Martin changed his mind about the project." She swallowed the names she wanted to call him. "He thinks it's too soon. I'm not sure what I'm going to do, probably return to the States." The idea of begging for her old job back made her nauseous. "But I don't want to leave."

A frown marred Cho Cho's forehead and then cleared. "I know who can help. He will know what to do."

***

The towering Shwedagon Pagoda was one of the oldest and most holy Buddhist temple complexes in the world. As Mallory stepped out of the car, she froze in awe at the sight of two immense chinthe, the mythical lions guarding the entrance to a vast shadowy stairwell.

"Come, Miss Mallory, we leave our phanat slippers here," said Cho Cho. "We must be barefoot to show our respect."

Mallory slipped off her sandals and added them to the

tumbling pile. "How will we recognize ours? Won't someone take them?"

"Oh, no! Bad karma to steal at such a sacred place. Come, we walk slowly. By noting each step, we clear our minds before we reach the top. This is the Eastern entrance – my favorite, very auspicious."

The stairway before them was broad and gritty underfoot, the ground deliciously cool. Mallory struggled to tame her thoughts and copied Cho Cho's mindful movement, carefully placing each foot before the next - not thinking about what might be lurking in the dirt under her bare toes. Ropes of black cobwebs festooned the towering timber roof. Massive lacquered support columns adorned with hand-hewn glass mosaics marched up the shaded walkway like a progression of painted giants. Devotional brass and gold leaf objects reflected and splintered glowing lamplight from small shops. Step after step, counting. One hundred and four, one and hundred five? She lost track. At the top, smiling women sold fresh flowers, incense, and sticks embellished with colored folded paper to be used as offerings at various shrines.

They stepped out of the murk into the brightness of the platform. A seated Buddha festooned with blinking fairy lights loomed before them. Several people kneeled or sat in various positions of prayer. Cho Cho guided Mallory to the left, joining a stream of people circumambulating the monument. A ribbon of marble tiles provided coolness underfoot. To their left, an intricately carved teak building sported multiple levels of wooden eves, all curving up toward the sky. Painted filigree motifs sprouted and spread like ivy, covering walls and ceilings. Images decorated every surface; bells tinkled and chimed in a cacophony for the senses. Everything was designed to lift the eye, the spirit, to the heavens.

People, young and old, attired in their colorful finest, smiled at her as they passed. A single monk draped in dark red glided by with lowered eyes. A dozen young nuns clothed in faded pink robes lined up from tallest to smallest perched on a step; the youngest no older than five. Folded white handkerchiefs protected their tender, shaved heads.

"Hla dey, hla dey," one girl called. "Very beautiful."

Mallory smiled at the sweet sight of the girls gawking and giggling into their hands. Cho Cho placed a small bouquet of purple asters into her hands and she inhaled the botanical fragrance of the flowers.

"I take you to visit my friend," Cho Cho said. "What day of the week are you born?"

"I was born in November but don't know the actual day of the week."

"Burmese astrology is different from the West. No matter, the weizza will know."

"What's a weizza?" Mallory asked cautiously. She wasn't in the mood for any more surprises.

"He is a famous wizard. We meet him now."

They slipped around a car-sized iron bell to find an ancient Bodhi tree surrounded by tendrils of roots spreading down through an opening in the marble tile of the platform. Bright silk scarves adorned both the trunk and branches.

"This is an important Thitpin Saung Nat shrine. Yokkaso is the name of the guardian spirit of trees. Nat worship is older than Buddhism in our country." Cho Cho held her hands together and knelt before the altar at the base. Touching her head to the ground before the tree, she rose and gestured for Mallory to follow her.

They entered an eerie space, like walking into a sound-proofed room. After the excitement and bustle on the other side, Mallory shivered in the sudden quiet. Even the usually raucous crows were still, the jet-black birds watching the two women with swiveling eyes. In front of them sat a bundle of rags. They walked closer, and the rags twitched. The pile was a living person, desiccated and bald.

Cho Cho bowed again and seated herself on a woven bamboo mat before the elder. "Come, Miss Mallory," she called.

"Please sit. This is Saya U Tha Aung. He is a powerful weizza, what we call a wizard astrologer. He can tell your future and what you must do for happiness."

The toothless man grinned as Mallory lowered herself to the ground and set the floral bouquet before him. He had blackish gums and sunken opaque eyes. "Is he blind?"

"He sees in ways we cannot understand."

The wizard spoke with a strange, high-pitched voice. Unfazed, Cho Cho murmured in reply, nodding her head.

"Give him your hands," she said.

Mallory raised her arms, uncertain if she wanted to be touched by the man. He snatched her wrists and yanked her closer. His claw-like fingers had long, sharp yellow nails. Stretching her hand flat, he traced the lines of first one palm and then the other. Nauseated by his breath and strange odor, Mallory tried to pull away but he held on with surprising strength until he released her. She surreptitiously wiped her hands on her skirt.

"Saya asks what is the day, month, and year of your birthday."

"November 7th, 1965."

With a nod, the wizard produced a battered black book and skimmed through the pages. He grabbed an old, yellowed composition notebook from under the mat and scribbled with a blunt pencil, giggling as he worked, pointing out each marking and symbol he drew, as if Mallory understood every word. Completed, he ripped the drawing from the book with a flourish and dropped the scrap of paper in her lap.

"What do I do with this?" Mallory asked, unwilling to touch the filthy paper.

The man leaned forward, opal eyes glowing, his face almost touching hers. A low-pitched humming seemed to come from all around them as he pointed his finger and, like a wood-pecker, tapped at her mother's necklace with the tip of a long nail. One. Two. Three. Mallory blinked. Behind her eyelids, she caught a flash of a polished wooden hallway. Doors lined the corridor, each marked with one of the wizard's drawn symbols. Then, an image of a man's back as he walked away from her into shadow. Mallory jumped when the old man began to speak again in his weird voice. Then he was still.

"What did he say?" she whispered.

Cho Cho shifted on the mat. "Saya said you are Sunday born. Day of the Geruda, a mythical bird. These people are very loving and lovable but also unlucky. He said you are making good dharma work, but an evil spirit, a ghost, has been following you for many lifetimes and causing mischief."

Mallory's necklace burned on her skin where the man had tapped. She felt an urge to rip it from her neck.

"Saya said much I don't know how to say in English," Cho Cho said. "He can fight this bad spirit, make it go away, but you must give him the special present."

Of course. Even magic has a price. "I guess he wants US dollars?"

"No! No dollars. He can make the spirit go away, make you lucky, but only this special present can make the spell."

"What *special* present?" Mallory had never enjoyed having her fortune told. She didn't trust anyone who said they knew more about her past or future than she did herself. There'd been stupid scenarios in her youth, playing with so-called magic eight balls or Ouija boards, where she thought she might learn something new about herself. Some bit of healing insight from her dead mother. But it always ended in disappointment. "I don't know about all this, Cho Cho. Let's just go..." She began to get up.

A sudden high-pitched keening filled her ears, the sound almost toppling her over in shock. A gust of cold air pushed her down and chilled the sweat on her face. Her skin rippled in goosebumps, and her ears popped like in an airplane.

"What the fuck was that?" Mallory touched her ears as the man stared at her expectantly, a combination of puppy and gargoyle.

"He is very powerful," Cho Cho murmured. "He says he will take your cursed necklace, and you will be free of the bad dharma."

Her mother's necklace? The man nodded as if he could read her mind. He poked at her with his wicked fingernail and giggled.

"No, Cho Cho, tell him I can't give him this particular present. It's all I have left of my mother."

The grinning man pulled an overripe banana from inside his shirt and traced a cross-hatched design on the soft skin with his fingernail. Holding the spoiled fruit out, he mimed eating. "Sa! Sa!"

She tried to push the fruit away, but with a whoosh, the strange rush of air returned. But not air this time. Something more. A shove from the hand of a giant. She watched her hand put the fruit into her mouth. Cloying sweetness coated her tongue and soothed her throat. The necklace blistered her skin. She yelped in pain and yanked at it. The old clasp pulled apart, and the pendant dropped to her lap. It lay like garbage – trash from the bottom of the bin. Something broke free in Mallory's chest, and she took the first deep breath in a long time.

"Ha! Yes, very good." The weizza nodded as he dropped the tawdry jewelry into his shirt pocket. With a shooing gesture, he indicated their audience was over.

CHAPTER SEVENTEEN

Geoffrey

Sarkies Bar in the Strand Hotel was quiet for a Saturday but it was still early. Geoffrey did his best not to flirt with the attractive barman. He was meeting Muang Chit later and didn't want to pollute his love for the young Burman. The bartender set down his gin and tonic with a bit more force than was strictly polite, sloshing a bit onto the bar. "And the cigarettes, dearie?" Geoffrey knew the young man rolled his eyes at him but it didn't matter. Nothing mattered but the ruby.

A murmur passed through the bar, and he glanced up to see Mallory enter. He remembered the first time he'd seen her, standing fierce and alone like a pale naiad before diving into the fray of the room. Like before, she caused heads to turn, but now there was something different about her. A hint of something spoiled and moldering, like a browning gardenia. He cringed. Women really were disgusting when they lost the shimmer of youth.

"Well, if it isn't my favorite chef, Mallory Jones." He pulled her face in for air-kissing. "Just the person I want to see."

"Wow, did I have an unusual day," she said. "Do you know anything about a famous astrologer who hangs out at the Shwedagon? According to my assistant, he's a wizard with special powers."

Geoffrey idly twirled the cigarettes the barman had finally brought. "Sure, many. Some are frauds who prey on tourists and gullible Burmese, but a few are the real thing, able to predict the future." His never-still gaze passed up and down the bar like a fly-fisherman casting his rod.

"Well, this guy didn't predict my future. He supposedly cast a spell to keep away a malign spirit that had been haunting me over many lifetimes." She cringed. "He made me eat a banana."

"Well, a banana isn't too horrible; it could have been something truly disgusting, like snake blood or maggots. What would you like to drink?"

"Whatever you're having," she said. "You're right. A banana wasn't so bad."

His eyes landed on a man sitting at the other end of the bar. "I should introduce you to Blake. He's the British commercial affairs officer. A little networking would do your project good."

The bartender set a tall gin and tonic before her, condensation slipping down the glass. She took a long swallow. "About the restaurant..." Geoffrey looked up at her tone. "It's been canceled."

"Canceled? But what happened, pet? How can that be?"

"Apparently, my asshole, douche bag of a boss had inside government information that changed his mind."

"Bollocks. What will you do?"

"I don't know yet." She slumped over the bar as if her bones had melted. "I have a little money but not enough to open my own place. I might have to leave Burma."

"But you just arrived, and I have so few friends." Geoffrey lit another cigarette, though the one he'd been smoking still smoldered in the ashtray. This new development might work out very well indeed. "I know. Let's plan a little trip, shall we? You can visit some of the tourist sites and have time for a good ponder. I would love to show you Mandalay Palace. We might make a weekend of it." He tried to scrub the pleading from his voice. "What do you think?"

Mallory yanked the hair tie from the back of her head and shook her head so her hair fell around her shoulders. Downing her gin and tonic, she raised a finger to order another. "Well, I've certainly got nothing else going on."

Geoffrey clapped his hand in delight. "But first, we're going to have a fabulous party to celebrate!"

"Celebrate my project's cancellation?"

"No, you noodle, celebrate whatever is coming next. Don't you know, the best prospects are always a surprise!" Geoffrey could attest to that, and he loved a party – especially when someone else paid for it. "Shall we organize something here, at the Strand?"

Her mouth twisted. "You know, I don't have an expense account anymore. I can't afford another three-hundred-dollar lunch. And who would I invite?"

"Hmm, let me think." He blew a series of smoke rings toward the ceiling, where they dissipated in the draft from the fans. "I have it! The evening before we travel to Mandalay, we'll hold a snack and cocktail party at your hotel. Nothing too over-the-top. We'll invite Jenny and your little assistant and, of course, Thierry. And anyone else you want. I might invite a dear friend, if you agree."

"And why do I want to do this?" She grabbed a cigarette from his pack and lit it with such ferocity he thought she might explode.

"Why not, my pet? Why not? Don't you know, parties are the civilized way to say sod-off to our grim past."

Geoffrey grew concerned when she laughed so hard, she choked on the smoke in her mouth.

CHAPTER EIGHTEEN

Mallory

Determined to see the tourist sights before she left Burma, Mallory hoped the Rangoon Recreational Park would provide a morning of distraction. But the small barren cages in the zoo told another story. The creatures appeared thin and sad; an elephant stood with her head pressed against the wall of her pen. A rhinoceros stood eating its own filth. She stopped before a caged lion – the once glorious creature had skinny flanks and a mangey coat. The pupils of his golden eyes were pinpricks of rage. She hated seeing animals in cages – all but one.

Mallory's father had lived in a similar cage at the Walla Walla State Penitentiary. When she'd turned eighteen and eligible to age out of the foster care system, she refused contact, not wanting her mother's murderer in her life. But after his release, he'd insisted on coming to her place of work, drinking endless cups of coffee until her shift was finished. He did that for over a week until he disappeared. No, she didn't know where he had gone, she told the police. Good riddance to bad rubbish.

Towering banks of black-hearted thunderclouds piled up in the Rangoon sky. She walked faster, outrunning ghosts, intent on reaching the other side of the park before it poured.

Picturesque Kandawgyi Lake appeared on the other side of the boulevard. A modest outdoor restaurant, little more than a smattering of tables and plastic stools, stood under the branches of a massive tree. The 'kitchen' consisted of a vast aluminum cauldron simmering over charcoal. Mallory was famished, but there were no available tables. She was surprised when a man, sitting alone, gave her a welcoming smile. "Please join me," he said in English.

"Thank you, but I don't want to intrude," she said.

"It is no intrusion. Do you like *mohinga*?" The man tilted his head toward the woman, fussing over the fire. A buzz-cut hairstyle framed his broad cheekbones giving him a vaguely military air. "My name is Zaw Wren."

Mallory hesitated for just a moment. It was unlikely he would spike her soup. "I'm Mallory Jones."

He adjusted a stool so she could sit. As she crouched down on the low seat, her skirt hiked up to her thighs. With a curse, she pulled it down. Something about knowing she was constantly being watched made her clumsy. She was growing tired of the constant scrutiny – what foolish thing would the Westerner do next? Maybe it *was* time to leave. She looked around and realized no one was looking.

"Where is your home? Are you a student?" The man was saying.

"I'm from the United States." The cook bustled over and asked her something in Burmese. Mallory only caught the word mohinga.

"What do you prefer in your soup," Zaw translated.

"Everything. I want to try it all."

A vigorous debate ensued between the man and the cook. At the conclusion, smiling and nodding, the woman hurried off to assemble Mallory's bowl.

"Have you tried any dishes other than Bamar?" Zaw Wren said.

"Isn't Burmese food all the same?"

"Oh no. We are a complex nation with many different people, all with their languages and customs, including food."

The woman returned with a steaming bowl of soup and noodles that reminded Mallory of the dish Cho Cho had arranged for her. But this was more savory and heavier on the fish sauce. Her eyes watered after taking a bite.

"Is it too spicy?" Zaw asked.

Mallory took a sip of tea. "No, this is fine. What is your favorite food?" His delicate wrists contrasted with his muscular forearms. She blushed for an instant as she imagined being wrapped in those arms.

"I am from Kachin State to the far north, so my preferred meals are from my homeland."

"How is it different from the food around here?"

"Kachin food is similar to Bamar but healthier. We use less oil and cook with many vegetables, often steaming our food instead of frying." He nudged the remains of fried chickpea fritters on his plate. "And we hunt meat from the forest."

"Meat from the forest...?" Visions of rabbit legs and venison steaks flashed through her mind, all nicely butchered and wrapped in white butcher paper with a string.

"Python, monkey, deer. Dried tiger is a delicacy..." Her jaw dropped as she imagined skinning a tiger. He quickly added, "That is the custom from the olden days. Things are different now, but some people in the mountain villages still follow the traditional ways. Do you not hunt in America for game?"

"Yes, we do." She'd prepared and cooked deer, elk, even wild grouse – searching for the little nuggets of shot that could crack a tooth – but animals from a zoo? "It's the tiger and monkey that surprised me. We don't have too many of those roaming wild in Washington State." She smiled. "But I've prepared my fair share of wild animals. I know some chefs that serve crocodile and snake, but I've never tried it. What does python taste like?"

"The meat is white in color, but the flavor depends on

what it eats in the jungle. It can be cut into steaks and cooked over the fire but is best when cooked longer. It can be chewy in texture. You like to cook?"

"Yes, I do. Or I used to." Mallory took another slurp of soup; the story of the failed restaurant could wait for another time. "What is your favorite thing to eat? Hopefully not tiger," she laughed.

"Hmm, let me think." He rubbed his hands through his short hair. "My favorite dish from home must be *hei jiao niu liu*. You can translate as pepper beef. The meat is boiled with hot peppercorns and pounded into flakes with fresh herbs. You are making me homesick, Miss Mallory." He said her name with a soft accent.

"That sounds delicious. Is there a restaurant where I can try it?"

"Not in Rangoon. You must travel to Myitkyina in the far north, I fear. Even eating certain kinds of food in Burma is a political act."

Mallory stopped chasing a crunchy bit of something delicious in her bowl and recalled Cho Cho's remarks about local people being watched when speaking with foreigners. She scanned the lakeside again. Most of the people she'd noticed after her earlier clumsy arrival had gone – she and Zaw were some of the last diners. But a solitary man sat half hidden behind the trunk of the tree, close enough to hear them if he wanted. He was so skinny and tall that he looked like an insect perched on the stool. He grinned when he realized Mallory was staring.

"I'm an idiot," she said. "I hope I haven't put you in any sort of trouble by talking to me."

Zaw's face hardened. He wasn't as young as she'd thought. "Burma is complicated. In my Kachin culture, guests are welcomed and are always treated with respect. Please don't be concerned about me. I would be honored to share the food of my homeland someday." He looked directly at the watching man as if daring him to do something. The man shrugged and turned his back to them but didn't budge. Zaw didn't seem to mind, so Mallory eventually forgot about him.

When Mallory asked what he did, Zaw chuckled and replied he was a repairman of broken promises. She shared the bare bones of the restaurant project that had brought her so far from home, refraining from the anger and frustration, not wanting to spoil the mood. Skipping along the surface, they spoke of Rangoon's notorious traffic and the surprising monsoon humidity that could grow mushrooms on shoes. Neither pressed the other for the details lurking under the surface like sharp stones that might disrupt the day's magic. Morning crept into afternoon as they talked. People came, ate, and departed. Most smiled at the foreigner sitting and eating like one of them.

Mallory wanted to see Zaw again. In the past, her track record for choosing men had been terrible. Thierry, case in point. But Zaw felt different. His gold-flecked brown eyes held no judgment, only compassion and curiosity. She wondered if there was a Mrs. Wren.

"Do you cook?" she asked. "I'm hosting a small gathering on Friday, and you might bring something unique to Kachin State?"

Zaw frowned and looked over at the dozing watcher Mallory had forgotten.

"Who is that guy?"

"An old friend," Zaw said cryptically.

She pulled a Bagan Inn business card and some kyats for the soup from her purse. "I enjoyed meeting you." She handed him some kyats for the mohinga and tea. "If you're interested in coming on Friday, please call me, and I'll give you directions to my hotel."

Zaw took the card but handed back the money. "I will try." As he stood, Mallory observed a physicality to him that hinted at agility and strength. He really was attractive. "Goodbye,

Mallory Jones. It has been my pleasure."

As she walked back toward the road, she kicked herself for not getting his phone number. Glancing back, she saw him striding toward the watching man's table.

Anger radiated from him like a swarm of hornets.

CHAPTER NINETEEN

Zaw

Colonel Zaw Wren surprised a sleeping watchman as he approached the entrance to the Bagan Inn. His superiors had approved his attendance at Mallory's private event but insisted he wore military attire to represent the Kachin Independence Army's mission. He felt conspicuous. "Don't worry, Grandfather," Zaw assured the startled old man. "I am expected."

When he'd first met Mallory at the lakeside restaurant, Zaw immediately recognized her as the Western woman he had seen at Bogyoke Market. He had invited her to sit with him without hesitation, surprising himself. He was a private man, lacking impetuousness, and he understood it made the other people at the restaurant apprehensive. Relations with foreigners were always suspect. But Zaw couldn't resist. Her eyes were the color of dark green jade, the precious stone of his homeland. He'd been more nervous than facing a battalion of troops on a battlefield when he had called her on the telephone. Thankfully, the reception was to be held at the Bagan Inn, not in a private home. In Zaw's experience, Christian Kachin Army colonels were not always welcome in ethnic Burman Buddhist homes.

The watchman hobbled after him in the gloaming dark until they reached the welcoming circle of light spilling into the garden. Zaw stepped across the threshold, gripping the tiffin box containing his food offering before him like a shield. He only saw Mallory laughing with a sound like springtime birdsong, her long neck tilted back, shining hair draped upon her shoulders. She was the most beautiful creature he had ever seen. He stepped further into the radiance of the room. Mallory spoke with an elegant Burman woman wearing a sparkling diamond necklace. He looked down at his humble uniform of green fatigues – Kachin army officers didn't wear glittering medals and fancy ribbons like the Burmese military.

"Zaw, you came!" Mallory exclaimed. "And in a uniform?" She held out her hand. Her fingers were slim and cool in the air-conditioned room. "This is Jenny," she introduced.

The woman stood only as tall as Zaw but gave the impression of looking down her nose. "Are you invading tonight, Colonel?" Her laugh sounded only half-joking.

"I apologize if I startled anyone. My chairman would only allow me to attend if I came in uniform." He handed Mallory the tiffin carrier. "Please accept this dish from my homeland. The mother of my adjutant prepared the food in Myitkyina and sent it on the train. I hope you enjoy it."

"Thank you. I'm sure we will." One of the servers relieved her of the container. "Come meet U Hlaing and Daw Sein. I told them you might join us."

Zaw spent much of his off-duty time in Rangoon in casual dress, walking amongst people without notice. But tonight, his insignia burned on his shoulder like a brand. He followed Mallory to a Burman elder settled on a wooden chair on the far side of the room. He was also formally attired and scrutinized Zaw myopically through thick, heavy-framed glasses. Next to him, his wife wore a traditional silk longyi but no jewels other than tiny jade buttons on her eingyi. A young woman, dressed more casually, was handing them a plate of fried beans.

"U Hlaing, this is the Kachin man I mentioned from the

lakeside restaurant earlier. I didn't know he was in the military."

The dignified man rose and adjusted his heavy glasses to peer at the insignia on Zaw's uniform. "I assume you are here for the peacekeeping accord?"

"Yes, I was recently commissioned."

"And this is Daw Sein." Mallory indicated the elderly woman. "She is a talented cook and helped me prepare some of the snacks for tonight. And their granddaughter, Cho Cho."

U Hlaing extended his hand in a firm grip; his eyes made huge by his lens magnification. He pulled Zaw close enough to smell the mothballs used to store his clothes. Zaw worried the man would ask him to leave, and he might lose any chance to know Mallory better. But the elder surprised him.

"Thank you, Colonel, for working to stop the fighting. Too many have been killed in this war between brothers."

"I agree," Zaw said, released from his anxiety and the Burman's bony fingers. "Unfortunately, in the name of self-determination," Zaw continued unthinkingly, "misdeeds have occurred. For decades, Kachin people have only wanted freedom from the rule of a government that loots our resources and muzzles our culture." He stopped, his words still ringing, mortified he had spoken too freely. "Please excuse my inappropriate words, Uncle. We are here to enjoy Miss Mallory and celebrate our similarities, not our painful history."

Zaw had no wish to antagonize his hosts and reminded himself to be more watchful. He wasn't in enemy territory, but the warrior in him understood that could change in a heartbeat.

During the exchange, Mallory had slipped to a linen-draped table in the center of the room, where two attendants arranged food and drinks. Zaw's pepper beef was now prominently displayed. She rang a fork against a glass to get everyone's attention. Two Western men Zaw had yet to meet sauntered closer, with a Burmese youth trailing behind.

"Thank you so much for attending our party," Mallory began. "Geoffrey thought it a good way to celebrate new beginnings." She smiled at the older man. "As most of you know, I came to Rangoon to open a restaurant. But, evidently, the universe has other plans for me. The guy who hired me turned out to be a jerk." Her words rustled through the room, the announcement a surprise to some of the guests. "I have no idea what I'm going to do next," she continued, "but my visa is good for another few weeks, so I plan to make the best of it." Her cheerful tone rang hollow to Zaw's ears. The Burman woman with the jewels looked particularly shocked.

Geoffrey put his arm around Mallory's waist. "Don't fret, dearie. Something marvelous is sure to appear. It always does, right, mon ami?" He looked at the other Westerner. "Let's toast to kicking out the old to make way for the new." He raised his glass and gulped his drink as if dying of thirst.

Uneasiness coursed through Zaw's body. Things were not as they seemed. It was unfortunate Mallory's project was canceled – it would have been pleasant to know her better – but there was something else in the room, something rotten. He looked at the doorway, wondering how long he would have to stay. After filling their plates, the guests sat in two groups. The Burmese gravitated toward one side of the room. The Westerners and the youth stood nearby. Zaw found himself in the middle, uncertain of where to sit.

"Sit with us, Zaw," Mallory laughed. "I can return the favor! Let me introduce my friends. Geoffrey Hughes works at the British Consulate, and this is his friend, Maung Chit. Thierry Aubert is a gem merchant visiting from France."

The Englishman held out his hand. Zaw tried not to recoil. The man's palms were soft as flowers. "How do you do? Are you from Rangoon?"

"No," Zaw said. "I come from the north." He had never spent time around foreigners other than Mallory at the lake. A smoky atmosphere of excess filled the room and he couldn't draw a deep breath.

"I'm about to try your Kachin beef." Mallory swallowed a bite. "Delicious." Her eyes began to water. "And spicy!"

Embarrassed he hadn't sampled the recipe in advance, he apologized. "Some cooks add hot chili to the black pepper for additional flavor. I should have warned you."

"No worries, I like it hot."

"Bonsoir, Colonel." The Frenchman's glance belied his polite greeting as he reached across Zaw to hand Mallory a glass of water that she ignored.

"Good evening." Zaw was now confident it was the man he'd seen slam the car door on Mallory. He wished his pistol was still attached to his belt, but the Tatmadaw had taken it away. He took a bite of the beef, chewed, and swallowed. The food tasted dry as paper.

"Kachin State? I would love to see the jade and ruby mines." Thierry set aside his almost untouched plate and lit a cigarette. "Are visitors allowed these days?"

"Not at this time. The mines are strategic assets." Zaw briefly considered explaining the complexities of Burma's natural resources to the foreigner, but Thierry interrupted him.

"You know, I am an expert on your rubies. My ancestor held the French gem commission with the Burmese king."

Zaw couldn't refrain from a jab at the officious man. "Then you know the best ruby mines are in Mogok of the Mandalay Division. Not Kachin."

"Oh?" The man's eyebrow lifted. It was evident he didn't like to be crossed.

The expression of disdain on Mallory's face when she looked at the Frenchman relieved Zaw's curiosity about their relationship. He continued, "There *are* some ruby mines in Kachin, but the quality is not as fine. In the springtime, they occasionally tumble down the Malikha River from the Hkakabo Razi Mountain. My father found one when he was young. He told me it was frozen fire from the heart of the mountain."

"Snow in Burma?" Geoffrey interjected.

"Yes, in the north. We border China and Tibet; we have high mountains with beautiful forests." Zaw imagined the dream place of his youth, not the hilly battlefields of his adulthood. Why was he in this room with these people? He became aware of U Hlaing's scrutiny from across the room. The old man fastidiously wiped his glasses and put them back on as if to see him better.

The elder rose and lifted his glass. "I wish to make a toast thanking Miss Mallory Jones. I am deeply saddened that she won't stay long in our country and open her restaurant. For to share food is the greatest of all peacemaking activities." He swallowed, sputtering as the whiskey went down his throat. "I have seen much in my long life." Daw Sein put her hand on her husband's arm and whispered, but he brushed her fingers aside. "I know of evil and wonder how loving-kindness and compassion can flourish in such poisoned soil. Each morning, I meditate and pray to Lord Buddha for guidance on counteracting the darkness. Then I go about my day; I wash my face and find, in the mirror, that darkness of which I speak." He blew his nose with a honking sound. "I apologize; I have had too much to drink."

Zaw held his breath, the room quiet enough to hear a gecko chirp. The granddaughter, Cho Cho, broke the spell, moving to help her grandfather sit.

The Englishman grabbed the almost empty whiskey bottle from the table. "Well, I'll drink twice to that," he said.

Mallory moved to kneel before U Hlaing. "I'm so sorry if this gathering brought you pain."

Zaw watched Mallory while the eyes of the Burman woman with the jeweled necklace followed him like a sniper.

"No, my dear. No pain, just the worry of an old man," U Hlaing said. "There is a desolate wind in my heart tonight. Thank you for this special evening. I hope we will meet again before you must leave. I know Cho Cho is very sad."

Mallory looked stricken as the granddaughter draped a

shawl around the plump shoulders of her grandmother. Tears had caused the floral motif of the young woman's thanaka to blend. "Cho Cho, let's meet after I return from my trip. I'm worried about what will happen to you."

"No need to worry about me," Cho Cho said. "We are survivors accustomed to disappointment." The woman's strong words rang in stark contrast to her tears. Zaw wondered what arrangement had been disrupted between Mallory and the Burmese family. Cho Cho helped her grandfather stand and then caught Zaw's eye at the door. She whispered, "My grandfather believes deeply in the peace accord."

"Thank you," he said. "Your grandfather is a remarkable man."

The peace agreement. That was Zaw's critical purpose. Not passing the time daydreaming about a pretty American. He knew better. Jenny also stood to leave. As Zaw watched Mallory's face fall yet again, he felt sorry for her. She had only wanted the support of her friends. The British man, who had been drinking heavily, giggled as he hand-fed the youth a tidbit of food.

The Frenchman opened another bottle of whiskey. "Let's toast to dry roads," he said.

Zaw shook his head no to the proffered whiskey. "Are you traveling?"

"Yes, we visit the old palace in Mandalay."

"Mandalay?" Zaw kept the surprise from his voice. He was also going to Mandalay in the morning.

Mallory returned with a smile that warmed him despite the freezing room. "You're traveling to Mandalay tomorrow?" he asked.

She glared daggers at Thierry. "Yes, for a change of pace," she said. "Geoffrey loves Burmese history and thought it would be fun to get out of Rangoon. We leave early in the morning." She looked in the direction of the giggling British man. "Hopefully."

It was time to abandon these foreigners to their dramas. Zaw couldn't bear to remain.

"Won't you stay for another drink?" said Mallory. "We didn't get a chance to talk much."

He held out his hand. "Thank you for a unique evening. I will remember it for a long time."

"It's been such a pleasure," she said. "I hope we can meet again someday."

Like the anticipation before a battle, a deep foreboding filled him as he put on his cap. The waiter rushed over with the washed tiffin box. At the door, Zaw said, "Mallory, if you ever require help for any reason, please contact me." He took a business card from his shirt pocket. "This is the phone for my office. Someone can always find me."

He fled into the night, his back tingling in anticipation of the bullet.

CHAPTER TWENTY

Mallory

Frogs bellowed like Tibetan monks in the warm predawn air as Mallory sipped a cup of sweet tea. Geoffrey's party to celebrate the end of her project had been a flop. What a shock when Zaw Wren had appeared in a military uniform – she probably wouldn't have invited him if she'd known. In hindsight, she should have found a more private way to say goodbye to everyone.

When Thierry had strolled through the door clutching a bottle of scotch and grinning like the cat that ate the canary, she'd wanted to strangle Geoffrey for inviting him along on their weekend jaunt. But after a few drinks and Thierry's solicitous apology, she calmed down, accustomed to men's apologies. Most of the evening, Thierry and Geoffrey had huddled in the corner like generals plotting an attack. She overheard a few intriguing words, but they'd changed the subject whenever she came near; she had yet to learn what this weekend getaway was really about.

Yellow headlights winked up the drive. Geoffrey grinned over the wheel of his dark green Land Rover as they pulled up to the hotel's entrance. Thierry rolled down the passenger side window. "Bonjour, Mademoiselle. Are you ready?"

"What the hell are you even doing here?" She threw her

overnight bag into the rear seat and climbed in. Thierry twisted around to ruffle her hair. Geoffrey had given some flimsy excuse about why Thierry was coming with them, but it had been late, and she hadn't paid attention. "Take it easy – my head is screaming."

Fittingly named, Highway One was the only major north-south highway in Burma, poetically referred to as the *Road to Mandalay* in novels and films. White pavement edge markers clicked past as they hurtled up the two-lane road. The solid wall of the night was broken only by the headlights of an oncoming vehicle, leaving them blinded as it passed.

Geoffrey chain-smoked, chattering about how his colleagues had advised him against driving north during the rainy season due to possible flooding. He claimed to have assuaged everyone's concern with the promise of souvenirs from Mandalay. His ambassador had taken him aside to reprimand him about the necessary protocol for a diplomat and remind him there wasn't enough time to register his out-of-capitol travel with the Burmese authorities. Geoffrey had assured his boss he would return before anyone noticed.

When he finally stopped talking, silence enveloped the car. Mallory dozed in the back, her head wrapped in a blanket, muffled against the cigarette smoke. She dreamt of her mother, only recognizable by the red glass necklace, a prize in a giant box of Crackerjacks. Over the years, the memory of her mother's face had dissolved like salt in boiling water. She woke and peered at the intermittent moon shining down at her with the wizard's black-gummed grin.

Night retreated in the sudden way of the tropics. After a few hours of driving, the landscape changed noticeably. Tall crops replaced the ubiquitous paddy fields. In the dawn light, Mallory could see miles and miles of sunflowers, tall heads pointed to the east, waiting for the sun. In need of a rest stop, Geoffrey pulled over to the side of the highway. He and Thierry stood behind the vehicle, facing away from the road.

Not wanting to drop her pants and bare her bottom for the world to see, Mallory grabbed her packet of tissues and stumbled down the verge in search of privacy. She walked to a dead tree about twenty yards away, poking through bushy peanut plants.

The tree's trunk was bone white, massive four-foot black fruit pods hanging from every branch. Mallory had no idea what sort of tree it might be but, preoccupied with relieving her full bladder, she turned her backside to it and lowered her jeans with relief. An odd susurration started that had nothing to do with the sound of her pattering urine. She tilted her face up to see one of the drooping things wriggling. It opened a bit, and two shiny onyx eyes blinked. With a screech, she fell forward, scrabbling away. All the other pods began to shiver and stretch leathery wings. She screamed, trapped in a horror movie.

First, to reach her, Thierry pulled her up by the armpits and dragged her away from the tree. "Ce qui se passe?" he bellowed.

Geoffrey followed close behind. "What the bloody hell are those?"

She pushed her face into Thierry's shoulder. "It's horrible," she sobbed.

"My lord," Geoffrey whispered. "Are they bats?"

"Bats?" She stared in disbelief. "But they're so huge." She disentangled herself from Thierry's arms.

"Actually, flying foxes," Geoffrey said. "I read about them; they're relatively harmless. They feed on fruit."

"Let's return to the car before we find out what they prefer to eat," Thierry said.

As they walked, her breath began to slow. "Who knew the Dracula legend came from Burma," she joked, but her pulse still throbbed in her throat. The sky cracked open as they crawled up the verge, drenching them instantly.

"Listen, I heard about a fried chicken restaurant not far

from here," Geoffrey said. "I think we can use a break and something to eat. Look for the road's junction heading west towards Mount Popa."

Mallory jumped into the car and shut the door with a satisfying thud. No six-foot bat could get in now. As Geoffrey started the engine, an overloaded public bus with drenched people crouching on the top roared past, almost shoving the Land Rover to the side in its watery wake. He set the wipers on high as he peered through the waterfall.

At long last, a faded mural of a chicken painted on the sagging side of a bamboo structure came into view. The rainstorm had passed, and the earth steamed under a weak sun. Mallory slid out of the car, still cautious about any unfamiliar wildlife. No animals in sight, but she spotted a cistern of water. "I have to get cleaned up," she said.

The men stood beside the vehicle, groaning and stretching. "I've heard the fried chicken here is delectable," she overheard Geoffrey remark as he and Thierry entered the restaurant.

She dabbed at the dirt on her pants where she'd fallen, but her tissues were no match for the sticky mud covering her knees. She laughed when she overheard Thierry's strident voice attempting to order.

"Chicken? *Poulet?*" he repeated, increasing in volume.

"What the hell, Thierry? She's not deaf," Mallory exclaimed. A teenage girl in a white tee shirt and a long braid down her back stood before him with eyes scrunched and head tilted to the side.

Hearing the commotion, an older woman appeared. "Welcome!" she exclaimed. "Please excuse my daughter."

"We're hoping to try some of your renowned fried chicken," said Geoffrey, ever the charmer.

The woman spoke rapidly to her daughter, who hurried to the back, presumably to place the order. The roadside diner was modest. Two sides stood open to the elements. Several dry tables covered with faded vinyl tablecloths had been moved next to the wall. "Do you have many customers here?" Mallory asked.

"Sometimes the bus stops or tourists come, like you," the woman smiled. "You go to Mandalay?"

Geoffrey settled himself at one end of a dry table. "Yes, we are. Do you have a menu?"

The woman chuckled. "No menu, sir. Only chicken. You want beer?"

"Yes, bring beer," Thierry said.

The proverbial light bulb went off in Mallory's mind. The concept of a one-specialty restaurant was not new – especially in Burma. Streetside vendors offered everything from deep-fried sparrows to pancakes, and the mohinga outdoor eateries were everywhere. What if a pop-up concept catered to a more international clientele?

"May I visit your kitchen?" she said. "I'm a cook, too, and would love to see how you set things up."

Delighted to show off her establishment, the owner took Mallory's hand like a long-lost friend and pulled her behind a wooden wall, chattering away in a mix of Burmese and English. The rain started again in a ferocious downpour, causing the tin roof to rattle and thunder. A man in faded green shorts and a singlet T-shirt sat on his haunches before a low wooden chopping block, dismembering chickens into small pieces with a giant cleaver. *Whack. Whack.* A tall woman stood by a massive wok suspended over an open charcoal fire, dropping bits of meat into hissing hot peanut oil. A young boy, about seven or eight years old, rinsed plastic plates from a single faucet, the dirty water running down a trench to the outside. It was apparent there was no government sanitation department to worry about.

"What spices are you using?"

"Turmeric and fish sauce." The woman pointed to a plastic jar of brilliant yellow powder. "We make a special sauce with tamarind from tree in garden."

"I can't wait to try it. Thank you for the tour."

She missed the simplicity of cooking – it was either delicious or it wasn't. There had to be a way to stay. She refused to return to Seattle with her tail between her legs, everyone thinking what a fool she'd been to leave. Begging for her job back was not an option, and fantasizing about sticking Martin with a hundred kabob skewers wasn't helping. She took a deep breath. Money was the key. She had Martin's envelope, though she doubted it would be enough, no matter how simple a restaurant. What if she could find investors?

Geoffrey and Thierry, their heads huddled, appeared to be deep in conversation when the thundering rain shower abruptly ceased. The only sound was water dripping from the bamboo eaves and the men's hushed voices. They didn't notice her watching.

"Yes," Thierry was saying. "Daw Khin Myint confirmed her cousin at the airport would look the other way when I go through security. She says it's not uncommon to smuggle jewels. Of course, she has no idea about the provenance of this particular gemstone."

Mallory slipped a bit closer, moving behind a refrigerator that hadn't worked since before the British occupation.

"How much will it cost to look the other way? How can we trust her?" Geoffrey's voice was unusually high-pitched.

"Three thousand US dollars and a promise to help sponsor her son at a French university. I trust her as much as possible, perhaps more than you."

"Let's just send it in the bloody diplomatic pouch? It's too risky."

"I told you. It stays with me..." Looking up, Thierry spotted her peeking from behind the fridge. "Mallory, ma chérie, what are you doing sneaking about? Is our meal ready?" He tugged her wrist close with surprising strength and put his lips against her ear as if he might bite it off. "Spying is not polite. Did you overhear our conversation?"

"Enough to know we're not visiting any palace." She yanked her arm back. "What are you guys up to?" The sweet dream about her own place vanished, replaced by confusion and apprehension.

Geoffrey fumbled to light a cigarette, dropping his gold lighter on the cement floor. "Bollocks." He scrambled under his chair to retrieve it and then lit his cigarette with shaking fingers. "Oh, hello?" he called out. "Can we have that cold beer now?"

The teenager appeared with a heaping platter of fried chicken, followed by her mother. The older woman grinned as she uncapped the Mandalay beer with her small, pointed teeth. The men were silent until she was out of earshot.

"Did I hurt your wrist?" Thierry's voice was silky gravel.

"What the fuck is going on?" She was angry. "Tell me now, or I'll go back to Rangoon on the next bus, and you guys can do whatever you want on your own."

"Please show me." He took her hand, but gently this time. He kissed the tender place where a nurse might take someone's pulse. "I'm sorry. We only want to keep you safe."

"Are you smugglers?"

"You know, sometimes it is better not to know," Thierry said. "Being too smart can be dangerous. Blame Geoffrey for inviting you." Geoffrey began to object but was silenced by a look and went back to munching his chicken. "I told you I was a gem broker, yes?" Thierry continued. "Well, a few years ago, a gem dealer in Bangkok told me a fairytale about a priceless ruby worn by queens for a thousand years. He claimed the jewel was real and owned by a private individual in Burma. Intrigued, I began to research the legend. With Geoffrey's help, I now know where to find it."

"This doesn't make any sense," Mallory said. "Why isn't such a valuable thing in a museum somewhere? Why would it

CHAPTER TWENTY-ONE
Geoffrey

Just after the town of Meiktila, Geoffrey screeched to a halt behind a stopped sedan in the middle of the highway. "Bloody hell." A line of stationary vehicles stretched for what looked like miles. "Guess this is what they warned me about," he muttered. "Wakey, wakey." He thumped his hands on the steering wheel. The long drive had lulled Thierry and Mallory into a hypnotic doze. "We have an unscheduled stop."

Thierry rolled down his window and gestured to a young boy walking along the shoulder, selling bottles of water and old newspapers. "What is the problem?"

The boy shrugged and held up a dirty plastic bottle. "One dolla?"

Thierry waved the child away and opened his door. "Mallory, shall we see what is happening?"

Rolling fields stretched on both sides to the horizon. A sliver of the sun sent down weak rays, slicing through the thick, steaming humidity. With traffic at a standstill, passengers exited their cars to stretch their legs, stopping to chat with strangers. An entrepreneurial peasant woman had set up a fried noodle stand and grinned with bright red betel-stained lips. No one seemed overly disturbed by the delay. Children raced past, playing a game of tag. They had driven into the midst of a bloody carnival.

Geoffrey joined the small huddle in front of the car. Mallory's face scrunched up to understand the blend of English and Burmese. "The bridge is out," she said. "It's crazy, but they say cars are being ferried on a raft across the washout one at a time. It might take all day. They don't know when it'll be fixed."

A Burmese man nodded vigorously, apparently satisfied with her explanation. "Yes, yes, very good." A small crowd had gathered to stare and offer advice. Geoffrey hated the passive scrutiny of the locals. He checked his pants were zipped.

Hussain, a truck driver dressed in gym shorts and white topi cap, introduced himself. He suggested they spend the night in Meiktila and wait out the road repair in more comfortable surroundings. He happened to have an uncle who owned a hotel allowing foreign guests.

"Putain," Thierry cursed. "There is no time for this nonsense."

Geoffrey clambered onto the hood of his Land Rover and put up his hand to shade his eyes. An endless line of vehicles was stalled before them. He hopped down, joints complaining. "We're buggered. We either wait it out, as the man suggests or turn around and return to Rangoon."

Mallory laughed as Thierry threw himself into the vehicle like a pouting child. "Well, okay then. Thank you, Hussain. Can you tell us how to find your uncle's hotel?" she asked.

"Perhaps better I show. I drive your English car?" he asked Geoffrey. "I am careful, good driver."

Exhausted from the long day, Geoffrey was ready to rest. He hadn't wanted to share driving the official vehicle with the others in case of an accident, but he was too tired to be bothered anymore. "All right," he told the man. "But what about your truck?"

Hussain laughed. "No worry, sir. My truck will not move for long time."

***

About seventy-five miles south of Mandalay, Meiktila sat on the crossroads of two important highways. Geoffrey had read how the Japanese flattened the town during WWII and rebuilt it with a unique, tourist-worthy central clock tower. Hussain stopped in front of the Happy Life Hotel, directly across from the famous landmark, and went into the lobby, calling his uncle to come and greet the new guests. The hotel was a splintering two-story wooden structure enclosed by a long veranda.

Geoffrey opened the Land Rover and let the young people take their bags. Ensuring the vehicle was secure, he followed them up the steps and into a dim lobby. Tall wooden shutters were closed against the rain, making it difficult to make out details of the room. A reception counter lurked at the rear. In the center, rattan chairs were arranged around a low teak table. God, he was sick of such dismal places. Paris was very far away, indeed. He cringed at the cobwebs hanging over his head from an unmoving ancient ceiling fan. The oppressive late afternoon heat made his balls itch with sweat.

A tiny Rumpelstiltskin of a man appeared. "Welcome, my friends. My name is U Rashid," he said. "Call me, Raz." Shaking their hands firmly, he added, "I am delighted you have come to my hotel. Please take sit, and rest while we prepare your rooms." With a booming voice, he called for someone to bring refreshments for their honored guests.

Geoffrey sagged into a chair, knees crackling. He wondered if he would be able to get up again without help. Mallory took the seat next to him. Thierry didn't sit, pacing the room's edges like a wild beast.

"Well, isn't this fun?" Geoffrey said to nobody in partic-ular.

Mallory hopped up when the truck driver re-entered the room.

"You will be comfortable here," he said. "I go now. My cousin give ride my truck."

"Thank you for your help," Mallory said. "You've been kind."

Hopefully, we're not all robbed in our sleep, Geoffrey thought. "Yes, thank you," he said aloud. "What can we pay you for your trouble?" He rummaged in his pocket. "I hope your truck is where you left it." It had been over two hours since they escaped the traffic jam.

"It is my pleasure to help," Hussain said, putting up his hand in a *stop* gesture. "Please, no pay."

Mallory knelt to open her bag and pulled out a Green Day T-shirt. "Please accept this gift."

Hussain's eyes grew round. "Oh, thank you, Miss." The truck driver took the shirt as if it were priceless – American pop culture items were valuable. "Thank you for kindness." He backed out the door.

"Where are we?" Thierry demanded after the truck driver was gone. "How far from Maymyo?"

Geoffrey began to reply when an ancient woman shuffled out from the shadows. She carried a loaded tray of teacups, packaged coffee mix, and a tall thermos of hot water. Rolling his eyes at the dingy state of the cups, Geoffrey opened the thermos. A whisper of steam added yet more dampness to his perspiring face. He had sweated through his shirt and wanted a shower more than anything else. He set the dented canister down and dug out his cigarettes.

He'd smoked almost half a pack before Raz returned. "I sorry for delay," the man said. He explained he had moved one of his guests from the honeymoon suite, as it was the only room with a double bed to accommodate the young couple. He hoped sir would be fine with a single room.

Mallory started. "But I want my own room. Three *single* rooms."

Raz's happy smile dropped. "I am sorry, Miss." He looked

to Thierry for confirmation and, not getting any, back at Mallory. "There are no more rooms. Perhaps the men can share the big room?"

Wouldn't that be a treat? Geoffrey changed his mind, seeing Thierry's grimace. The Frenchman had hated him since they'd first met. He chuckled. Blackmailing him and having his father kidnapped to help him get the ruby probably hadn't helped either.

"Oh, all right," Mallory said. "If I don't shower soon, I might kill someone."

"Hopefully it won't come to that," Geoffrey said.

"We'll see. The night is young."

Paperwork complete, Raz took their passports, explaining it was standard procedure, and promised to keep them secure. Geoffrey wondered what the safe might look like; probably a drawer in a cabinet. Following their host up the wooden steps, he half expected to run into the relocated guests prowling the hall, but the dark corridor unfolded before them in eerie silence. Mallory gasped as if in recognition of something but remained quiet.

The room was pitiful. The bed was hard as stone, and a cockroach, the size of his fist, guarded the shower. Geoffrey wondered where Maung Chit was at that moment, probably with some younger, good-looking man. Jealousy was an ugly emotion for an old man, but dreaming of a shared life was all that remained.

He wasn't surprised when Costa had blackmailed him in Paris with photographs taken in a private club, cavorting with leather-clad young men. Geoffrey knew better. It would have cost him his career, so he fled to the remote posting in Burma, hoping Maurice Costa would forget about him. But the gangster never forgot.

Now, finding the ruby was the only way to be free.

CHAPTER TWENTY-TWO

Mallory

Thierry cajoled the hotel room door open with the antiquated key. "Et, voila!"

"Do you expect applause?" Mallory pushed past and lobbed her bag on the bed.

The long wait for their rooms had tested her already limited patience – she was particularly irritated she had to share a room. She was hot and tired and regretted not turning around at the chicken stand and returning to Rangoon. "Explain it to me again." She plopped on the edge of the bed and plucked at the dried mud on her jeans. "You and Geoffrey are in cahoots to steal an ancient ruby. How can I be *camouflage*?"

"I told you everything in the car." Mallory heard the denigration in his voice as if she were stupid. "If the authorities are watching, traveling as a group makes us less obvious. We don't know if the government knows about the ruby, but they would be interested if they knew it was in the country."

"Who hired you? Why don't you steal it for yourselves?"

"I tell you again – Maurice Costa is a powerful international gangster with eyes everywhere."

"What's your connection to him, and how does *he* know about the ruby?"

"I am stinking with sweat, and it is a complicated story."

Thierry stood and unbuttoned his shirt. "Let's shower and cool off a bit?"

She crushed crumbling bits of dirt in her palm and let the dust fall to the wood floor. "Okay, but I'm going first."

Naked, under the feeble flow of rusty water, she slid a bar of soap under her armpits and between her legs in the tiny adjacent bathroom. The water was warm, probably from sitting in a water tank on the roof, but it was wet. Eyes shut tight, she lathered her hair.

"Quelle belle fille," said Thierry with his sexy accent. "May I join you before the water is gone?"

Eyes stinging from soap, she flipped her hair back and glared. He stood in the doorway, tall and naked and muscled in all the right places. "Get out," she hissed.

"I wish to apologize."

"For what?"

"For whatever you wish."

"If you want to be nice, then leave and let me finish my shower."

He put up his hands in a placating fashion. "Okay, okay. I only thought we might have a little fun as we are stuck in this shithole together."

Still dripping with soap, she grabbed the handkerchief of a towel. As she tried to squeeze past, Thierry grabbed her like at the chicken stand, but this time, his grip was a vice. He shoved her against the wall of the shower and put his lips against her ear. "Do you really want to play hard to get?" As he spoke, he put a knee between her legs, forcing them apart. His fingers tangled in her public hair as if he could open her like a safe, his erection pulsing against her belly.

"Let me go." A horrible memory surfaced as she pushed back against his slippery chest. Beery, cigarette breath. Heavy limbs holding her down. *No, no, Daddy.*

"You will change your mind," Thierry whispered. He ran his fingers across her neck and down her breasts. "Just like you did with that pitiful necklace."

She pushed past him with a shove and entered the bedroom. She stood dripping onto the wooden floor. Back in the bathroom, Thierry was muttering in French. She crouched, trying not to cry aloud. The veiled threat, the pain in her wrist, a man's unwanted erection. More memories rose — faded Polaroid pictures from her past. A split-level Centralia Washington house surrounded by dead grass. The yeasty odor of empty beer bottles. Ash-covered plates overflowing with cigarette butts. The muffled thud of a fist. The sound of weeping, so much weeping.

Her mother leaned over a chocolate cake. "Can I blow out the candles, Momma?"

But pretty Momma wasn't smiling. "Can we just get this over with?" Mommy glared at Daddy. "You're already drunk."

"Come on, Rachel. Donbesucha bitch." Daddy's words slurred together, but Mallory recognized the naughty word. "I got you somethin' special."

Daddy fumbled in his pockets and retrieved a necklace with a sparkling red stone. He tried to stand to put it around Mommy's neck, but she pushed him away. He stumbled and almost fell. "Doncha like it?" he appealed.

"Fuck off with your pawn shop trash." Momma's eyes squinted. A tear splashed down. And another. She took the necklace and smashed it into the cake. "How's that? Huh?"

Mallory hid behind the refrigerator as Daddy knocked Mommy to the floor.

The next day, her mother was dead, and her father incarcerated for life. A policewoman found the necklace still buried in the stale cake. The officer had washed it off and given it to the social worker. "A little girl should have something nice to remember her mother."

A generator fired up at the rear of the Meiktila hotel. With a squeal, the ceiling fan began to churn the stifling air. Mal returned to the bathroom. "If you touch me again, I'll kill you," she whispered in Thierry's ear. She grabbed his testicles. "Do you believe me?"

"Yes," he gasped.

"I'm only in this for the money."

***

Stepping out on the long veranda of the hotel, Mallory glanced up and down the town's central street. The watch tower stood before them like a ridiculous multi-tiered wedding cake in the violet twilight.

Raz pointed them in the direction of a restaurant. "It's not far, sirs. Just down and left. Tell them you are my guests, and they will take care of you —the owner is my cousin."

"Well, off we go!" Geoffrey laughed, seemingly oblivious to any tension between his friends. He put his arm through Mallory's and guided her down the wooden steps. "Isn't it grand that everyone in this town is related? One big happy family."

They dodged light traffic, stumbling along the roadway. A curious dog followed close on their heels until Thierry threw a rock to chase him away with a yelp. The sky went black like someone had thrown a switch. The restaurant was typical, with a concrete pad, open sides, and a tin roof. A chubby man with massive forearms crashed pots and pans over a fire in the simple kitchen. "Welcome!" he called as they stepped under the buzzing lights. "Please sit."

A repurposed metal sign promoting men's hair pomade topped the table. Mallory sat close to Geoffrey, tracing circular burn marks seared into the advertisement with her fingertip. Her wrist throbbed. Thierry sat opposite. Above them, a fluorescent light strip swarmed with moths.

The chef bustled over with a stained towel flung across one shoulder. "I make excellent biriyani for you? Mutton outstanding."

"Thank you, yes, three servings of the *plat du jour*," Geoffrey said.

"And beer," Thierry said.

"Sorry, sir," the cook said. "We sell no beer. But I send the boy to get from shop?"

"Just bring us something cold," Thierry grumbled.

The man spoke rapidly to a young boy sitting at another table with a skeleton-thin old man wearing a skullcap. He handed the boy some kyats, and the child ran into the night.

"Why don't they offer beer?"

"This is a Muslim establishment," Geoffrey said. "At least they are accommodating."

Wearing welder-sized gloves, the cook placed a narrow-mouthed, squat pot on the table, which explained the round burn marks. He dug into the mixture with an aluminum spoon, blending the layers of meat and aromatic basmati rice tinted bright yellow with turmeric and saffron. She took a small bite. And then a bigger one. The owner bustled around their table, clearing dishes and shooing away curious, gawking locals. Geckos scampered across the ceiling, gorging on their own perfect meal of mosquitos, fat with the foreigners' blood.

"How do you two know each other?" Mallory asked after the effects of her second bottle of Mandalay beer had softened the edges.

"From Paris," Geoffrey leaned forward as if to whisper. "We are *dear* old friends." His bitter tone told her otherwise as Thierry rolled his eyes.

"Tell me more about this ruby. Is it really that precious?"

Thierry poured more beer into his glass. "It is possibly the most valuable Burmese ruby in history. Certainly, the most famous. I learned about it two years ago and have followed its trail ever since."

"How did *you* get involved with this scheme?" she asked Geoffrey as he lit yet another cigarette.

"Blackmail." He blew a smoke ring toward the buzzing

light. "Luckily, a little birdie chirped some valuable information into my pillow. If we are successful, I'll be free for life."

"And you?" she directed to Thierry. Filled with mutton and hate, she couldn't look him in the face.

"As I told you, this man Costa is very dangerous. He collects misery to use against people like chips in a Monaco casino. For almost two months, he holds my father for ransom. I don't know if he is alive or dead." Thierry pointed a cigarette at Geoffrey. "No thanks to him. I don't know why he threatens Geoffrey, but I can imagine."

"Shut up," Geoffrey hissed. "You don't know anything."

"What does he mean?" she stared at Geoffrey. "Are you really a diplomat?"

"Ask the professional jewel thief."

She looked at Thierry for the first time since the shower. "Your father was kidnapped?"

"Yes, to ensure I help him," he snarled. "Costa agreed to pay a substantial finder's fee plus my father's release." He pointed his cigarette again at Geoffrey. "And whatever debt he's holding over our friend's head."

"What do I get for helping you?"

"It all depends on Geoffrey's contact and if I can steal it. Then we must smuggle it out of this damned country."

"Where is it now?"

Geoffrey began to reply, but Thierry shushed him to silence. The cook sat nearby; his head tilted as if listening.

***

They left Meiktila after an unsatisfactory breakfast of instant coffee and rubbery eggs. Mallory had passed the night counting minutes, curled on the edge of the bed, as far from Thierry as possible. The traffic jam of the previous day was gone, the repaired bridge sprouting like a nighttime mushroom.

"Until the next big rain," Geoffrey sneered as he circumvented a deep rut on the highway.

At the outskirts of Mandalay, they dodged bicyclists and bullock carts and an elephant crossing the road, cradling a colossal teak log in its muddy trunks. Mallory tried to snatch a peek of the royal palace in the hazy distance, but only caught the faraway top of Mandalay Hill. They started up the steep highway, the route switching back and forth up an escarpment, climbing over three thousand feet above the valley floor in a few short miles.

To pass the time, Geoffrey recounted a ghostly anecdote about their destination. "Candacraig Hotel in the town of Maymyo has offered British colonial society relief from Rangoon's sweltering summer heat for over a hundred years. It's uncertain how many spirits haunt the place," he said, "but the most notorious is a young woman in Victorian dress seen playing the piano. Not perturbed by ghosts, George Orwell is rumored to have written *Burmese Days* while staying there, pouring out his hate for the empire like notes from a possessed piano."

Geoffrey slapped the steering wheel. "I would have had much in common with dear Mr. Orwell. For Crown and Country and all that rot, ha-ha!" He eased the Land Rover close to the edge of the precipice as he passed a heavily-loaded truck carrying potatoes wrapped in burlap bags. "The ghost is thought to have been the young wife of a prominent civil servant who fell in love with a local man. Incensed that her lover was Burmese, the Scotsman supposedly strangled her to death one hot evening when the club ran out of ice for his gin. I heard the locals still refuse to clean the rooms alone."

Mallory was noncommittal in her opinion about ghosts. Though, after her experience at the Shwedagon pagoda, a ghost playing the piano didn't seem impossible. The click, click tapping of the wizard's fingertip on her necklace still echoed in her head. To shut out the scene in the shower with Thierry from her mind, she daydreamed about what she would do with the proceeds from the sale of the ruby. Staying in Rangoon might be nice. But if there was as much money as

Thierry intimated she could go anywhere. Do anything. *Don't be such a fool*, said a voice in her mind. *They have no intention of sharing the money.*

Maymyo was a beautiful hill town famous for strawberries and a botanical garden that rivaled Kew Gardens in London. In the town center, they stopped before a formidable clock tower where the words *Purcell Tower* gleamed in golden paint.

"The Burmese seem to have a remarkable desire to know the time," Thierry commented.

"A residue from us Brits, always trying to control the unruly masses," Geoffrey said as he took another wrong turn.

Finally, a turret-adorned red brick building appeared at the end of a long, muddy drive. A man of Indian descent wearing longyi and a black wool waistcoat came onto the veranda. "Hello. I am Joseph, manager of Candacraig."

He led them into an expansive foyer with a sweeping staircase. An old piano stood in the corner. To the left, they entered a small reception area where they surrendered their passports and filled out forms in triplicate. After promising them a proper British meal of shepherd's pie, Joseph invited them to sit on the veranda for drinks. Deep rattan chairs hinted at another era. A young woman brought a tray laden with crystal glasses, and bottles of club soda and Johnny Walker Red. A young boy, about ten years old, scurried around, lighting incense coils at their feet to keep mosquitos at bay.

Mallory's eyes roamed the beautiful vista as she sipped her whiskey. The estate's edges became indistinct and then lost in the deepening twilight. Dreams were simple. She only needed money. *Hush little baby, don't say a word, Momma's gonna buy you a mocking bird*, sang her mother's voice.

"Not such a bad life." Geoffrey blew a perfect smoke ring.

"As long as you're the one drinking the whiskey." Thierry stood and paced to the other end of the porch. Pivoting back, he peered into the entry. With a shrug, he sat back down. "We can talk."

"Now what?" Mallory asked.

"We make contact." Thierry topped his glass. "Right, Geoffrey?"

"Well, first, we stay and enjoy our dinner, of course."

Mallory followed Geoffrey's gaze to the small, wide-eyed boy crouching in the shadow.

CHAPTER TWENTY-THREE

Thierry

The hotel slept – he hoped. The staircase was smooth and polished, but every second step creaked. Thierry knew to keep his center of gravity low with flexed knees and tight core, but still, he wondered who might hear him. He wanted to retrieve their documents before slipping away from the hotel. No questions from curious hotel managers that could alert authorities. Just tourists wanting an early start on their way back to Mandalay.

He scoffed at the unlocked reception door but then remembered where he was. In a police state, no one breaks the law. Hadn't he told Mallory that? Still, he was a testament to the fact that criminals were everywhere. He flicked his cigarette lighter to get his bearings in the pitch-black room. The locked drawer would only take a second to open. As he jiggled his pick, he heard a noise. Not a sound so much as an exhalation of air. Hair on his arms and the back of his neck stood up. He had to take the risk to ensure no one else lurked in the room. Flicking the flame again, he scanned the small space. Nothing. He unlocked the drawer and pulled out two passports. After a moment, he took out the third. He couldn't leave her behind as he and Geoffrey had planned.

The sound came again. Louder now, just outside the door. Thierry held his breath as he eased open the door, but the moonlit foyer remained empty. Shadows poured down the sweeping stairwell from the inky-dark upstairs landing. The first few notes of Debussy's *Clair de Lune* crawled up his spine. Thierry recognized the detested music Janice Landry had insisted he listen ad nauseam. The sound trickled out of the dark and pooled around his ankles, tripping him as he galloped back up the stairs.

An hour before daybreak, Thierry tapped on Geoffrey's door. "It's time. Where's the boy?"

"With the car." Geoffrey's voice was a ragged whisper. "What is she doing here?" He pointed at Mallory.

"Keep quiet," Thierry growled.

For a moment, he thought he heard the murmur of music again, but it was only his banging heart as they tiptoed down the steps and eased out the front door. A tiny firefly of flame winked alive in the hand of the boy beside the Range Rover. They climbed into the car. Geoffrey released the brake, and the vehicle began to roll soundlessly down the drive. Thierry looked back. A woman stood in the entryway, outlined in a faint blue glow, her hand lifted in a wave. He blinked, and she vanished.

Geoffrey glared in the rearview mirror at the boy. "Are you sure you know where to find this monk?"

"Yes, Saya, I know." The boy cringed in his seat. "My cousin tell me. I take you. You give me dollars." The previous evening, he'd told them that the Venerable Thakin Sayadaw kept special magic hidden deep in the forest about ten miles outside of Maymyo in a Buddhist monastery.

It should have been easy to find, but locating the monastery on the remote road took longer than planned. Little more than an unpaved path led deeper into the forest. Geoffrey cursed as he ground the clutch, dodging massive teak trees suddenly illuminated by the Range Rover's yellow headlights, the boy pointing the way. It was apparent few people traveled the remote route.

When they finally arrived, dawn glowed in bits of sky peeking through the dense forest – too light for Thierry to attempt to enter unseen. The four stood in a circle – a pitiful coven of would-be thieves.

"Now what?" Geoffrey put his hand on the boy's thin shoulder and peered into his triangular face.

"No problem," the boy said. "I find Sayadaw." He wriggled out from beneath Geoffrey's hand and sprinted away toward the wooden gate of the compound.

"You fool," Thierry said to Geoffrey. "We find the place while everyone is sleeping, you said. The kid shows me where to search, you said. Easy as pie, you said." He stuffed his fists into his pockets, afraid he might pummel the Englishman in frustration. "Do you think the monk will just hand it over if I ask nicely?" He pulled his hands out and took a step toward Geoffrey.

"Let's see what the little one can find out," Mallory said. "We're here now."

"Don't be so foolish, Mallory. We will spend the rest of our lives in prison. We should leave now."

"Give it a few more minutes, mon ami," Geoffrey said.

"If you call me your friend again, I will kill you."

"Quiet. Listen," Mallory said.

The sound of monks chanting morning prayers reached them as the wood smoke smell of cooking fires filled their noses. A colossal teak tree leaf twirled down like a falling helicopter and landed with a dry crackle. Thierry leaned back against the car. The urge to smash Geoffrey's face and grab his keys subsided. There was nothing to be done but wait.

After long minutes had passed, the boy reappeared. "Come. Sayadaw ready now. No shoe."

Barefoot, they hobbled toward the rough-hewn gate. Thierry winced as he stepped on a small stone. Though the path was muddy, dead leaves crunched underfoot. A teakwood building stained a faded blood-red loomed before them. The two-tiered tin roof held carvings shaped into flickering flames. Several smaller buildings surrounded the larger structure. A half-naked monk pulling water from the well for his morning bath ignored them. The chanting had stopped; the only sound was the creak of the well's rope.

The boy led them up a sturdy, short ladder into the expansive interior of the building. Thierry felt like he had climbed into a medieval spaceship hovering above the ground. Shutters dimmed the light, and the place appeared to be empty. But as his eyes adjusted, he discerned a frail monk in dark red robes seated on a cushion in the middle of the swept floor. The monk waved them close to sit before him. He was smiling as if at long-lost friends.

"I've been waiting for you." He spoke English with an upper-class British accent.

Thierry and Geoffrey exchanged quick looks. "How could you have been expecting us? Did the boy talk?" Geoffrey reached to grab the boy's arm.

"No, no. Please leave the child. He is only doing what I asked of him." The man sighed. "I have carried this burden for too long, alone. Be patient, have some tea, and I will tell my story." He nodded to the boy, who scampered off.

It crossed Thierry's mind that the child had been sent to call the police, but they hadn't done anything wrong - yet.

Rows of burning incense sticks created a low-lying aromatic haze. A larger-than-life, gold-leafed Buddha figure shimmered in the dusky light. The fingertips of the seated statue's right hand touched the red lacquer dais upon which it sat. Mallory's smoky emerald eyes glinted within the frame of her pale face. Time stopped as they waited for the tea. The room, the monastery, and the forest were quiet, waiting for something portentous. The heat grew unbearable.

A shaved head appeared over the ladder. In a crouch, the bathing monk deposited a tray of teacups before the Sayadaw. He bowed three times and crept back the way he had come.

The boy followed with a steaming kettle.

"I have lived in this forest," the monk finally began, "since the assassination of Aung San, our beloved leader, in July 1947. I came to this forgotten monastery to keep the evil you seek hidden and my people safe."

"What evil is that?" Geoffrey said.

"Patience," the monk admonished and then sipped tea. "When my friend Ko Aung San was still alive, we fought the British as part of a group called the Thirty Comrades – *Thakin*. We shared a desire to see British rule overthrown and the egalitarian principles of communism ensconced."

Thierry's attention began to wander. The wretched heat and humidity weighed his drooping head. He hadn't slept well since Mallory's threat, half expecting to find her standing at the side of his bed with an ax. The monk's voice carried a hypnotic resonance. *One. Two. Three.* Thierry counted the bars of illumination cast by pale sunlight staggering across the polished floor.

"One evening, in preparation for battle," the monk continued, "we partook of the ancient Burmese military ceremony of *thway thauk*. A doctor drew blood from each of us and poured it into a traditional silver bowl. Pledging eternal loyalty, each comrade drank. Aung San revealed a vast, perfect, heart-shaped ruby. Its rays flashed around the room like a dazzling sun. *Let this stone represent the eternal heart of our homeland,* he said. Then, he passed the jewel for each man to touch and hold. He explained it had been a gift of good faith by our Japanese ally, Emperor Hirohito..."

Suddenly, Thierry gasped. Across the room, a woman's slender white foot, toenails painted a deep crimson, extended into the splinter of light. The color of the polish was familiar.

"...Hirohito wished the ruby to return to its original home, just as the Thirty Comrades would return power and control to the Burmese people. When my turn came to hold the jewel, a chill made me shiver, and I passed it quickly to the comrade beside me. I feared a malevolent vibration followed the gem, and I worried for our cause if such a thing represented us."

Thierry jerked awake and attempted to contain his excitement – the monk was talking about the Heart Stone. He glanced at Geoffrey, who was staring at the monk as if at a teacher in a classroom. Mallory's eyes were watching the corner where he had seen the foot. Her mouth looked pinched as if she'd eaten something sour.

"The next day," the monk said, "Japan began its invasion of Burma with the firebombing of Rangoon and troops advanced from the east through the Thai jungle, the Thirty Comrades at the forefront. The unprepared British were trapped unawares in the bloodbath."

"Where was the ruby during the invasion?" Geoffrey asked.

The Sayadaw ignored him and continued his story. "It wasn't long before Aung San became disillusioned by Japan's promises of independence. Flipping sides, we joined with British forces and turned against Japan, ultimately helping the Allied forces. I blamed it on the ruby, as nothing but treachery had come since it arrived."

Mallory's eyes shifted from the corner to meet Thierry's. She curled her lips.

"...I was proved right when armed men broke into the Secretariat Building in downtown Rangoon and Aung San was gunned down by spies financed by the very same British we had helped. Deceit, lies, and layers of treachery. I realized the stone was dangerous and mustn't fall into the wrong hands. It had the power to cause harm and disruption, magnifying the worst in susceptible souls. I took it and fled here."

The old man shuddered, exhausted from his long speech. The boy poured him more tea, which he gulped.

"Do you know why we are here?" Thierry wrenched his eyes away from Mallory.

"Of course, I know why you are here," the Sayadaw exclaimed. "Many years ago, I first held the secret in my hands and knew it for what it was – temptation and evil. But so very valuable. I kept it hidden from the generals during the dark decades of their rule, and now that Aung San's daughter has returned, it must be taken away from our home so she can govern fairly and our dear land might prosper again. The jewel that once honored Lord Buddha was perverted from its true purpose when it was stolen for greed. I had hoped to keep it safe for all time, but the temptation is becoming too strong. It eats at me with the cancer of desire." He began to laugh. "Don't you understand? I invited you here to take it from me!"

"You're going to just give it to us?"

"Yes. But you must promise to take it far away so it never returns."

"No worries about that, mate," Geoffrey smirked.

Thierry couldn't believe his ears. The foot with toes painted in his mother's favorite color had never been there. He shook himself wide awake. "Where is the stone now?"

"I hid it near Anisakan Waterfall. I'll show you. And then you leave me to the peace of Lord Buddha and my own dharma."

Grasping a gnarled stick, the monk rose and hobbled to the door.

CHAPTER TWENTY-FOUR

Mallory

Mallory raced barefoot through dried teak leaves back to the Land Rover. The sound of someone following, crashing, right behind. But no one was there. *Slow down, take a breath.* She leaned against the car, hand on her knees. The musty smell of unopened rooms caught up and filled her nose.

Geoffrey opened the door. "Come on, let's go!"

Thakin Sayadaw climbed in the front. She sat in the back with Thierry, the boy between them. Bumps in the path caused them to sway. The silence was interrupted only by the monk's occasional direction. Reaching the paved road, they sped past Purcell's Tower and turned west toward the village of Anisakan. Geoffrey's profile radiated focus. Equal parts fear of disappointment and expectation grew until Mallory thought she would be sick. She cracked open the window. The Sayadaw began to chant. She hoped he prayed for them all.

Soon, a train-like rumble filled the car. She opened her window to the roar of thundering water. Following the monk's knobby pointed finger, Geoffrey shifted into four-wheel drive and turned on a dirt path that followed the edge of a precipitous gorge. Giant glossy philodendron and rubber tree plants clutched at the vehicle as it snaked down. Yellow orchids stood out like vivid stars against the dense green.

At the end of the track, unable to go farther, Geoffrey switched off the ignition. He swiveled to face Thierry with a terrifying grin. "Okay, *mon ami?*"

Mist drenched their faces and dampened their clothes. The boy helped the monk down from his seat. After arranging his robes, the Sayadaw gestured they follow him as he labored up a slick rocky trail using his stick in one hand and the boy's shoulder in the other. Hundreds of feet above their heads, the deafening waterfall plunged over the ridge.

Edging around the rim of a pool, they dipped behind a curtain of water into a hidden grotto carved by thousands of years of tumbling, irresistible force. Tree roots twined sinuously out and into the earth. The boom of the cascade created a physical vibration. Shrines of gilded Buddha figures decked with floral offerings and sodden incense filled the dim space. Mallory jumped at the sight of a glistening black statue with staring white eyes perched like a gargoyle near the entrance. It looked exactly like the weizza from Rangoon.

"Now what?" Geoffrey shouted over the sound of the water.

"After I give you the stone," the Sayadaw said, "the child and I leave. Do what you want with it, but you must go and never return."

"Agreed." Thierry wiped water from his eyes.

Reaching into his cloth bag, the monk withdrew a flashlight and scrambled deeper into the rear of the cave. He stopped to bow before an alabaster Buddha covered in a lush patina of moss. Thierry helped him push aside the heavy statue, revealing a secret niche in the rock. Shining light into the darkness, the monk tugged out a silver box, black with tarnish.

"Mon Dieu."

"Open it!" Geoffrey shouted.

Thierry opened the box and revealed a bundle wrapped in shreds of silk. Letting the fabric drop, he discovered another smaller lacquer box the size of a pack of cigarettes. He levered off the lid and gasped as a massive ruby rolled into his palm.

"Holy shit..." Mallory couldn't believe her eyes as she filled with fizzy, ridiculous hope. It was true.

Thierry held it up. "Shine the flashlight here."

"Is it real? Is it the one?" The cords on Geoffrey's neck stood out.

Thierry released a sigh. "Yes, I think it is."

Geoffrey reached out and snatched the jewel. He squeezed it in his fist and put it against his lips. "Oh, you beauty!"

Thierry grabbed it back. "I need better light."

Consumed by a compulsion to hold it herself, Mallory inched forward. The wizard's dry cackle tickled her ear. The obsidian statue grinned down from its perch.

"You have what you want." The Sayadaw's voice was firm. "We leave."

Mallory almost tripped over the boy, trembling from fear and cold. "My dollars," he wept.

"Not so fast. We can't have you sharing secrets, now, can we?" Geoffrey pulled the old monk's arm, causing him to trip on his robes and tumble to the ground. A wicked-looking knife appeared in the Englishman's hand. He crouched. "No talky-talky for you."

The Sayadaw put his palm against Geoffrey's chest. "It is your dharma now."

Geoffrey pushed him back. "Shut up, you stupid bugger." The blade glinted in the low light before disappearing into the old man's throat.

The boy shrieked and threw himself against Mallory. "What the fuck, Geoffrey!"

"Grab the lad, Thierry. Don't let him get away!" Geoffrey shouted.

Thierry gaped. "What are you doing? He gave it to us."

The boy pulled away and knelt by the monk, a great sob shaking his narrow shoulders, the revered monk little more than a tangled pile of robes.

Geoffrey got up, brushing at the muck on his knees. "Bollocks, this suit is ruined."

Mallory put her hand over her mouth to hold back a scream. It was all happening so fast. Another knife, another fist, stabbing again and again, but the hand holding the knife had been hers.

With a roar, Thierry shoved him against the wet stone of the cave. He wrenched the knife from Geoffrey's fingers and, clutching him in an embrace, thrust it up and under the ribs of the Englishman, "How do you like that, *mon ami*?"

Heart pierced by the blade, Geoffrey slumped to the wet earth, scarlet blossoming across his linen jacket. Unsure whether she wanted to weep or laugh at the unfolding horror, Mal bit down hard on her hand. His suit was definitely ruined now. Her body tingled with adrenaline as she tasted her own blood.

Thierry pushed his hair from his face, leaving a smear of gore, black in the feeble light. He bent to pick up the box, then retched. The smell of blood saturated the small space.

The boy squatted nearby, his face pale with shock. "You give me dollars," he sobbed.

Mal had witnessed violence in her life – heard the crack of a palm striking a woman's face, the thud of a boot kicking a fallen body; seen a corpse filleted like a trout. She knew shock's slow-motion dilation of time. Elastic as a rubber band, expansive as a balloon, then the laser focus. The bubble would pop. The clock was ticking. *Tick-tock.* Where was the ruby?

"How much were you supposed to pay the boy?"

Thierry stepped away from Geoffrey's dead body, his face green. "One thousand dollars." He drew an envelope from his back pocket and shoved it at the child.

The boy recoiled from the bloody envelope. Mal grabbed it, pulled out the notes, and crouched down so she could feel his panting breath. "What's your name?"

The boy's wide eyes turned to her. "Naing," he hiccupped with fear.

"How old are you, Naing?"

"Eleven years." His shudders lessened, soothed by her calm voice.

"Bad things happened today, Naing." Her face inches from the child. White surrounded the brown iris of his eyes. "But you're a big boy, right? We must forget and not tell anyone, okay?" She placed fingertips over the galloping heart in his chest. "You have to hide this secret." She widened her smile. "Who else knows about the monk and the ruby?"

Naing's eyes swiveled to Thierry and back. "My cousin in Rangoon. He boyfriend to..." He glanced at Geoffrey's body.

Mal leaned closer. So much depended on soothing the child and ensuring he wouldn't talk. "Your cousin will be happy with the money. He will be very proud of you." She held out the small bundle of one-hundred-dollar bills. "Take it." Her voice became stern as she whispered into his ear. "But, Naing, this is our special secret. You don't want something else bad to happen, right?"

The boy's head bobbed in understanding as he snatched the proffered notes and ran out through the water. The sound of his slapping footsteps faded in the waterfall's thunder.

"Why did you let him go?" Thierry said.

"Really? Were you going to kill the child, too?"

His stained hands dropped to his sides. "No, of course not. We must conceal..." He gestured at the dead bodies.

"Where's the ruby?"

"Later. There's no time for that now. Help me hide them."

Rage filled her as she recognized that all-too-familiar tone of condescension. Why do men think they know the answers?

"Help me!" Thierry huffed as he hefted Geoffrey's shoulders. "Take his feet."

The ground was too rocky to bury them, and the pool too shallow. After long minutes of strenuous pushing and pulling, they concealed the bodies behind rock outcroppings. No one would find them unless they knew where to search. She hoped the Burmese authorities didn't have crime evidence processing units.

Outside the cave, Thierry wrenched open the back of the Land Rover and grabbed their bags. "Hurry!" he hissed. His head swiveled, looking for witnesses. "Wash off the mud."

They stripped off their mucky clothes. Thierry's nakedness glistened as he stood under the waterfall. Generations of noble ancestry forged into undeniable handsomeness, no hint of a stain. *Hurry, hurry,* Mal said to herself as they dressed in fresh clothing, stuffing their soiled garments into Geoffrey's valise. Who knew how often people visited the remote shrine? They had to get away.

"Where are we going?"

Thierry grimaced as he familiarized himself with the controls of the vehicle. "Rangoon. We must go as fast as possible before the monk's absence is noticed." He ground the clutch. "Let's hope the boy will keep his mouth closed long enough." At the top of the ravine, he turned right. "This way to Mandalay?"

"Can I hold it now?" She stared at his profile.

"Mon Dieu, Mallory, be quiet and let me think."

Who are you to tell me what to do? Mal was the balloon, filled to almost bursting, the tension excruciating. "Do you think a thing can make someone evil or amplify what is already there?"

"What are you talking about?"

"The stone, the ruby." Mal shouted. Cracks were widening.

"What does that have to do with anything? We're in a bad situation; we remain calm and think clearly. We make the plan. I contact Daw Khin Myint. We need plane tickets. I need a phone..."

"I want to see it now!" She slammed her fist on the dashboard. "If you want my help, you'll hand it over."

Thierry swerved to the side of the road. "All right, all right, calme toi!"

He pulled the box out of his pocket. It appeared old, chipped in places, with bamboo and horsetail showing through the black lacquer and gold leaf. Prying off the lid, she tipped the ruby into her palm. It fit perfectly. A pretty heart from a fairytale, drawn by a child, translucent as crimson amber. She squinted to see if she could see through it, searching for any strange hint of supernatural power. The jewel was clear but had an intimation of a smile within its depths, like the moon that sometimes looks like a woman's face. Rutile? The cracks that let in the light. The weizza's whispering was silent. Maybe there'd been no promise of magic. Any sorcery was of her own making.

Halfway down the escarpment, Thierry pulled over to take a piss. A heavy-weighted truck lumbered up the hill toward them and then passed. Thierry stood with his back to Mallory, the city of Mandalay in the hazy distance – the nondescript silhouette of any man with fists.

Mal slid into the driver's seat and started the engine. Thierry glanced around in surprise, his mouth a small O. Clutch in gear, she pushed the accelerator. The tires spun a moment, and then the car rammed into him with a dull thud. He fell. Attempted to stand. She backed up and hit the gas again.

Thierry slept – a handsome French prince – bright ribbons of blood running from a wound in his broken head. A nearby stone had bits of brain stuck to it. It was quiet except for the far-away grinding of the truck's gears as it made its way up the steep hill. Silence for a long moment, as if underwater. A shuddering breath, numbing herself to do what was next. His head bumped and turned as she tugged him to the cliff. She closed his eyes with a bloody fingertip and then heaved him over the edge.

Back in the Land Rover, she wiped her hands on her skirt and adjusted her empty rearview mirror.

CHAPTER TWENTY-FIVE

Mallory

Mallory parked next to the Candacraig Hotel. Only a few hours had passed since they'd first crept away in the early dark. Soaked in sour sweat, she pried her hands from the steering wheel and stepped out of the vehicle. The garden glowed and pulsed around her; pink bougainvillea stung her eyes as tiny gardenias from nearby bushes assaulted her with their funereal perfume.

Joseph loomed on the steps. "I assumed you checked out earlier. Your passports were gone." His earlier courteous tone was replaced by something sterner.

"We didn't want to bother you. Is my room still available?"

Joseph glanced at the muddy Land Rover and back to her. "Are the others coming later?"

"No, just me." Could he see the blood stains on her shirt, the mud on her skirt? "They went back to Rangoon. Catching the train in Mandalay."

His eyes narrowed, but his burnished face stayed smooth. He snapped his fingers to call the house boy to fetch her luggage from the car.

Her teeth began to chatter. "I'll grab my bag myself." Thierry and Geoffrey's cases remained in the back. She should have thrown them out along the way. Breathe. Did she have her passport? "Can I check in later? I want to wash and rest a little. It's been a long day already."

Joseph gazed up at the morning sky. "I'll put you in a single room."

She locked the room door, sat on the bed, then got up again to ensure the door was secure. Someone was playing the piano, and the soothing music calmed her banging heart. With a zip, she opened her travel bag. The small lacquer box remained safe, but she sought something else. And then she saw it, a glint of white paper – Colonel Zaw Wren's business card.

Crows roosting in the trees outside the window woke her from a deep nap with their raucous party noise. Showered and dressed in fresh underwear, she tucked the ruby into the stretchy fabric of a sports bra. A loose-fitting blouse camouflaged the bump. As she headed downstairs for food, a faint echo of the earlier music lingered like old perfume. The ebony piano gleamed. Goosebumps rose along her arms.

Joseph stepped out from the shadow of the back hallway. "Would you like dinner?" he inquired. "The cook made a traditional Sunday roast."

"That sounds fine."

Mallory hadn't expected to have any appetite, but the dinner was delicious; the garlic-studded mutton roasted until tender with crispy potatoes and fresh mint sauce from the herb garden. An older English couple were the only other guests. When Joseph brought her a second glass of claret, Mallory asked if he would sit with her for a moment. He drew a chair from a nearby table and sat, obviously uncomfortable with the familiarity. His earlier stand-offish tone had shifted back to polite courtesy.

"How may I help you?"

"I'm in a bit of a bind," she spoke softly so as not to be overheard. "My friends left without me. They took a taxi to the airport in Mandalay."

"That's rather unusual. What can I do?"

She placed Zaw's business card on the linen tablecloth. "Would you please help me reach this man?"

Joseph read aloud, "Colonel Zaw Wren, Kachin Independence Army, Liaison to Myanmar Peacekeeping?"

"Yes, I met him in Rangoon, and he offered to assist me with any problems on this trip. I won't detail my situation, but I know he can help."

The manager gazed across the room – eyes hooded with discomfort. She knew calling someone in the military might bring unwanted attention, but she had no choice.

"I'll see what I can do," he said. "There are no telephones in the rooms. But I'll let you know when I've reached him, and you can speak in the office."

"Thank you, Joseph. I'm sure you understand this is a confidential matter."

"Of course, Miss Jones. At Candacraig, we pride ourselves on our guests' privacy."

"By the way, who was playing the piano earlier?" Mallory imagined a Victorian woman with a spine so stiff she might shatter.

His polite smile dissolved. "No one here plays." He rose to greet the other guests, making no further mention of music.

Alone in her tower room that night, Mallory watched a gecko hunt for his dinner while she waited for the ghost to serenade her again. But the piano remained mute.

Sometime during the night, the sound of a creaking chair woke her. A pale blue glow lit the room, and Thierry sat on a wooden rocker in the corner. He smiled and nodded so she could see the horrible wound on his head. It began to bleed again, and he put his hand up to his face with a moan. She jumped out of bed and grabbed a towel from the bathroom. "Thierry, are you okay?" she cried. "I thought you were dead." She pressed the cloth to his head and watched it turn black. With a gasp, she woke up.

But she was tumbling down the side of a volcano over and over, sky, dirt, sky, with stones and roots gouging her body until she rested against a tree trunk and then woke for real. She lay unmoving, staring at Thierry's empty corner until dawn broke open the day.

At breakfast, Joseph told Mallory he had spoken with Zaw Wren's adjutant. The Colonel was in Mandalay for an ethnic minority summit. The assistant would pass on the message to call Miss Mallory Jones at the Candacraig Hotel at his earliest convenience.

She settled on the porch to wait, ruby in her hands, rolling it back and forth, not thinking about nightmares, murder, or a gemstone's corrupting influence. She only admired the radiance and marveled at how such a beautiful thing could grow deep in the depths of the earth.

And how big a lie would it take to keep it?

CHAPTER TWENTY-SIX

Zaw

Zaw reread the note, thinking there must be some mistake. He was mentally exhausted after a morning spent navigating the political minefield of consensus gathering amongst groups that had hated each other for generations. For the thousandth time, he reminded himself he was not a diplomat, but in the untenable position of having to act like one.

When he saw Mallory Jones's name on the message, his breath caught in surprise. Embarrassed by his reaction, he glanced around to gauge who might have noticed. She needed *his* help. When he'd seen her surrounded by friends, he'd been impressed by the Burmese who trusted her, especially the elder, U Hlaing. Zaw doubted such a man would be an ally of the American if she were unworthy. The other foreigners were another issue. He wasn't surprised she required help if the French gem merchant or British diplomat were involved. Perhaps he would be foolish to come to her assistance. But after a day such as he'd had, something was appealing about the simplicity of helping one person, one woman, versus a country that had been tied in knots for decades. As he walked back into the next round of meetings, he asked his aide to order a car.

That evening, Zaw sped to Maymyo. As usual, the phones

were down during the rainy season, so he could not reach her hotel. He prayed Mallory was safe and speculated on the nature of her emergency. His training kicked in as he prepared a checklist of potential problems and contingencies – none of them good. Halfway up the escarpment, another option appeared. Perhaps she wanted to see him again? In the short time since meeting Mallory Jones, he thought of her often. The tilt of her head while she spoke. The instant he had walked through the door and heard her laughter. He chided himself for such weakness, but the memories would unfold again, not prepared for the effect she caused in the uncultivated part of his soul where love for a woman might dwell. For a man accustomed to the realities of war and life on the battlefield surrounded by other men, she had entered his bloodstream like malaria.

Darkness engulfed him as the car drove away, and Zaw stared at the colonial relic. The hotel had been challenging to find and, as the minutes had ticked past, cruising futilely up one wrong lane and down another, the potential for tragedy amplified in his imagination.

Someone called his name from the veranda. Mallory sat in the corner, illuminated by a circle of golden candlelight, an almost empty bottle of scotch by her side.

"Thank God you got my message." Her voice was hoarse.

"What happened?"

She gestured to a deep rattan chair. "They're all dead, Zaw."

"I don't understand," he lowered himself next to her. "What do you mean?"

"Thierry and Geoffrey and the old monk."

Fear jolted. He whispered. "What are you saying, Mallory? What monk? How can they all be dead?"

"Because of this." She hovered her fist over Zaw's hand until he opened his fingers, and then she let something drop.

He angled the object toward the burning candle. It winked in the soft light as if alive, and he let it fall to the table with a thud in alarm. "What is it?"

She scooped it back and took a deep breath. "It's a priceless ruby from Catherine the Great that Thierry and Geoffrey were trying to steal from an old monk, but he gave it to them in a cave behind a waterfall where Geoffrey went nuts and murdered him, which made Thierry crazy, so he killed Geoffrey." She took another breath. "And then Thierry fell off a cliff."

Stunned to silence, Zaw stared at the woman before him, wondering if her mind was sound. But how to explain the stone?

He took her hands between his palms. "I'm here now. We'll find a solution together." He used the tone of voice he might use when speaking to a skittish horse. "Have you eaten today?"

"Maybe something at breakfast."

"Let's get you some supper." He helped her to her feet.

He averted his eyes as she plucked the ruby from the table and slipped it under her blouse. There would be terrible consequences if even a bit of what she had said were true. Such a jewel could only bring disaster. His hand still prickled from the stone's brief touch.

Wide-eyed at the appearance of a hungry Kachin army colonel holding the hand of his American guest, the hotel manager retired to the kitchen to make them sandwiches. Zaw understood that even an empty room could have ears, so he led Mallory outside to the garden. Clouds swiveled overhead, revealing random stars and a gibbous moon. He gently guided her through retelling the previous day's events, often stopping to clarify individual details as they paced back and forth. Her story was astounding. Unbelievable. But it was evident something traumatic had occurred.

"Where was this monastery?" he asked for the second time.

"Not that far from here," Mallory's voice was increasingly sharp as she told the story again.

"And the Sayadaw kept the ruby secret all this time?" It wasn't unheard of for a revered monk to have treasure, but this particular stone was unusual. And the fact he wanted to give the gem to foreigners? Unlikely. However, it was all too believable that the Western men would murder to possess the valuable jewel. But Mallory?

"Yes, I already told you."

"And the Frenchman. Tell me again."

Mallory turned her face up to the night sky. Zaw couldn't tell if she wept. "It was a terrible accident." Her voice cracked. "He slipped and fell."

"How did you all know about the ruby?"

"It was Thierry and Geoffrey. They had made some arrangements with the monk. I knew nothing about it until I saw it in the cave."

What a predicament. Every instinct warned Zaw to retreat and leave her to her fate. The woman was caught in a tangle of poor judgment. But she had pried open a part of his inner self he didn't even know existed. Guilt.

***

After the Myitkyina executions, Zaw had lived with self-condemnation for months, breathing guilt with each breath and drinking it with every sip of water. Death was assumed during wartime. But the killing of children was another matter.

Decades of poppy cultivation in Zaw's homeland had led to an explosion of drug abuse; opium used for centuries for medicinal purposes became abused for profit. Diseases spread on shared syringes, and families were destroyed. Out of desperation, the local leadership enacted the Three Strikes program. Anyone guilty of a drug offense – minor or not – would have one 'strike' against them. If convicted of a third 'strike,' the offender would be executed by firing squad.

Three teenage boys worked in the Hpakan jade mines and, like many, used opium as an analgesic after long, excruciating hours of digging for the precious ore. One evening, they shared a pipe and had the bad luck of being seen by an informer. Their mothers – local religious leaders – and the village headman spoke before the council. But there could be no exceptions. It was their third strike.

On the day of the execution, dozens of people came to bear witness. Women wept, and men stood tall with their ceremonial swords. Of the five soldiers chosen to carry out the sentence, only three reported for duty. Colonel Zaw Wren and another officer had to stand in. Soldiers lashed the boys' wrists and ankles to the corners of heavy wooden beams. From the scope of Zaw's rifle, they appeared crucified.

Zaw saw those teenagers' drooping bodies every night before he slept. Could helping Mallory be a chance for atonement? Or was he only convincing himself for other, more personal reasons? He needed more time. "It's not safe here," he finally said. The killing of a monk was unthinkable, and the Burmese authorities would come seeking vengeance. "I must find someplace safe for you."

"I can't go back to Rangoon."

"You will return the ruby to the monastery?"

"Are you kidding?" She put her face close to his. "That jewel is my first chance at a good life on my own terms. Please understand. I gambled everything to come to this country. There's nothing left for me at home."

Air hissed from between his teeth. "I must think."

They ate their sandwiches in silence. The walls of the empty dining room leaned in to listen. The hotel manager wasn't in the room, but Zaw knew he was waiting nearby.

"Will you help me?" Her voice was pitiful.

A picture came to mind from childhood: a tattered English language workbook where a prince on a white horse rescues a princess from an ogre. It was the first time Zaw had learned of people with yellow hair and skin as pale as snow.

"I will take you someplace safe while I investigate."

"I don't care where I go as long as I keep this." She touched the spot over her heart.

"That makes it doubly dangerous."

"I know."

Zaw swallowed harsh words. The ruby made everything that much more treacherous. A stone like that is noticed. Someone must be searching for it. Could he escape with her to his ancestral village and disappear forever? He admonished himself to stop imagining such foolishness. He needed time, and there wasn't any. There was only one option.

"Take your belongings," he said. "We leave now."

Mallory's steps pattered up the stairs. The manager appeared. "What is happening with the foreign woman?" He spoke Burmese. "Will there be trouble?"

"The authorities will come," Zaw admitted. "I suggest you forget my visit and plead ignorance. The tourists left abruptly without stating their destination."

***

The British vehicle was grander than anything Zaw had driven before, but still, he maneuvered cautiously, his shoulders hunched around his ears. The narrow winding highway unrolled before them in the Land Rover's high beams – the thin, muddy shoulder the only landmark to guide him from plunging off the edge into a valley below.

Mallory broke the silence. "Where are we going?"

"We're heading north on the Lashio Road to Hsipaw." Zaw gripped the steering wheel. "Do you believe in fate?"

"Maybe." Her hands knotted in her lap. "A lot of bizarre things have happened since I came here. Is it fate? I don't know."

The road unraveled in the dark. "Mallory." He glanced over to see her staring at him. "The only solution is for you to cross the Thai border by foot. Then, in Chiang Mai, you ask the American Consulate for help, telling them a story about how you lost your passport. Then, you must leave Thailand immediately. I don't know how closely Burma and Thailand share information, but missing foreigners – especially a British diplomat – will be significant news for the entire region."

"What about the ruby? Can I take it out, too?"

Illuminated by the glow from the control panel, he could see the soft roundness of her lips. She caught him looking, and he glanced away.

"Precious gems have been smuggled from Burma as long as there have been generals and kings." He prayed she would give up her obsession with retaining the stone, but he knew the powerful draw of such a fortune. Desire. Zaw was beginning to understand the emotion.

It was close to midnight when they reached Hsipaw. Inching down the deserted street, he told Mallory to watch for a faded Pepsi advertisement. Shop after silent shop lined the way, made of dark wood with rusting metal roofs. It seemed they were the only people alive. Finally, he spied a familiar building on the outskirts of town.

"Get in the back," he said. "No one must see you."

He got out and knocked softly on the front entrance. After several long minutes, a sleepy older woman appeared, holding a lamp. Her head swiveled up and down the empty street. "Why are you here?" she whisper-hissed, voice laced with fear.

"You once promised me help if I needed it. The time has come to fulfill your obligation."

With a quick glare at the unfamiliar vehicle, the woman stepped aside and let him enter. The shop was dim, illuminated by another lamp in the corner. Shelves piled with dusty homewares lined the walls. A graying man wearing a blue and green checked longyi stood in the narrow space clutching the edges of his tattered orange cardigan. A girl sat wide-eyed on a bamboo sleeping mat.

The woman shut and locked the door. "I did. But that was long ago." She spoke softly in Jing paw, the familiar tones a balm to Zaw's heavy heart. He hated involving the family who he had helped escape from the aftermath of a terrible battle many years before, but he was desperate.

"I want you to hide someone in your store room for a few days, a week at most. I wouldn't ask if it wasn't critically important."

The man's back was stooped so low he had to twist his neck to meet Zaw's eyes. He said, "We do as you ask, Colonel."

The woman whimpered in fear but nodded yes. Obligation was a currency more valuable than money.

Zaw crept back to the car and tapped on the window. "Come, Mallory."

Her head jerked up. "Where..."

He shushed her to silence. Shutting the car door with a soft click, he led her through the shophouse into a back store room. The woman held the lantern aloft. Shadows crept across the walls. The man and girl turned their faces to the wall.

"These people will keep you safe until I can arrange a way to smuggle you across the border."

"How long do you think?"

"I don't know, Mallory. Most important is to deal with the vehicle. It's a beacon for the authorities, especially with the diplomatic license plate. I must do this before daylight and then report to my chairman. I have been gone a long time."

"Why did the others turn away from me?" Mallory eyed the woman, staring at her as if at a wild animal.

"They can answer truthfully they didn't see any foreign woman."

"Why would anybody ask about me here?"

He shook his head. "The police will interrogate everyone, everywhere, about you. We must be faster than them. Do not leave this room. There is a toilet behind that door. Do you understand?"

"I'll be quiet as a mouse."

Zaw left her alone in the tiny room with only the lantern, several dusty cases of bootleg Pepsi, and a priceless ruby for company. He had never been so frightened in his life.

CHAPTER TWENTY-SEVEN

Mallory

Daylight shone through cracks in the bamboo wall. The claustrophobic room held only a mat on the dirt floor and a woven screen hiding the stinking latrine. Light crawled across the ground, shifting from white to gold as the hours passed and the heat grew. The woman didn't come, and Mallory's thirst became intense.

She slipped the jewel from her bra and held it to the sunlight. The stone came alive, and she imagined the queens who had worn it with pride and the armies that had fought to keep it safe. The hint of a smile winked from its depths. But as the light transformed to indigo and nighttime returned, it degenerated back to mere mineral. Corundum. An accident of geology. With the twilight, her emotions devolved into dread. She'd come to Burma to fulfill a dream but was now trapped in a nightmare. *Stupid girl, stupid girl.* The ruby was only as precious as the money it brought.

The door finally rattled, and the woman entered, bringing a thin cotton blanket, a towel, and a bit of soap. Mallory grabbed the water bottle from her hand and gulped it down in relief. The woman backed out and immediately returned with the first of many bowls of noodles.

Hours became days. Mallory slept on the narrow mat, her

arm the only pillow. She squatted over a wood plank in the latrine outside and sluiced away the waste with rainwater from a rusted oil drum. It was difficult to separate the monotony of awareness from the drowsy somnolence of half-sleep as she waited and tried to keep her mind as blank as the sky. But memories are insistent mosquitos. The frenzy and violence of the grotto behind the waterfall flickered on a loop. Again and again, the monk collapsed to the ground. Geoffrey's linen suit bloomed crimson red. Thierry's brains baked in the sun. The ruby made a tiny sound like a chuckle, and she dropped it in surprise. It rolled into the corner and winked.

Murder was easy. Mal hadn't planned it, though she'd fantasized about it for years. But when her father knelt before her, hangdog expression, begging for forgiveness, she'd only pitied him. He'd been waiting in the dark alley behind the diner where she worked. From the corner of her eye, the man's silhouette seemed familiar, but she couldn't see clearly in the dim diffused light emanating from the volcanic ash on the ground two weeks after the eruption of Mount Saint Helens. The mountain had exploded sideways, covering the region with an estimated five hundred and twenty tons of pulverized rock turned to fluffy ash vomited up from the center of the earth.

As she hefted the bulging garbage bag into the dumpster, he'd rushed toward her. She'd panicked, dropping and spilling the contents onto the pavement.

"I'm so sorry. I only wanted to help," the man said.

"I got it." Mallory knelt on the slick ground, incensed she had to pick up the disgusting garbage. It had been a long shift deep-frying chicken and french fries for the rich university kids who swarmed the restaurant after the bars closed.

He dropped to his knees, scraping chicken bones and greasy napkins into a pile. "Mallory." He said her name like a prayer. "I'm so sorry."

Mal's head jerked up. He was older, of course, and not as

thin as when he'd been a crackhead alcoholic. The prison had made him healthy. Given him new teeth, too, she noted as he sank back on his haunches and smiled.

"I've missed you." His voice trembled.

To her dismay, he began to cry, big fat tears blubbering down the sides of his nose. "What are you doing here?" His release date, marked in a black Sharpie on her bathroom mirror, was still months away.

"They let me out early. I couldn't miss your birthday."

"Right. So, the Washington State Penitentiary cares about my birthday?"

"I missed so many." He pleaded for forgiveness.

She stared at him. "They gave me Mommy's necklace, you know."

"Necklace? What necklace?" As he wept, snot ran from his nose.

"Right, you were too drunk to remember, I guess."

"Oh, sweetheart," he sobbed.

"I'm not your sweetheart."

She grabbed the knife she kept in her back pocket. His eyes went wide. She shoved it, over and over, into his flabby stomach. *Bye-bye, Daddy.*

***

Zaw returned during the dead of night on the sixth day. Mallory woke, blinking in the lantern's glare. "You're back?"

"Yes." His voice slumped in exhaustion.

"Can we go to Thailand now?"

"We have to get to the border first. Put on these clothes. Be sure to wrap your hair and hide it under the cap. Cover the bottom of your face with the scarf."

After changing into faded fatigues, she found Zaw in the main room. The woman and her family were gone.

He shrugged at the sight of her. "I hope it's enough to

disguise you. Don't speak to anyone. There are no Westerners where we're going. The two men outside are our guides. They are not good men, but I have no choice. They are smugglers and soldiers from Khun Sa's insurgent Mong Tai Army, and he has loaned them to me. Khun Sa calls himself a Shan nationalist, but he is nothing more than a drug dealer. I promised him a seat at the peacekeeping negotiations table in Rangoon in exchange for his aid, which gives him more status than he deserves." Zaw peered closely at her with questioning eyes. "The bodies from the cave are still missing, but a driver discovered the Frenchman two days ago."

Unconsciously, she touched the bump of the ruby under her shirt and pulled her fingers away when Zaw frowned.

"You must hide in the back of the truck with the cargo. There will be checkpoints. It is hazardous."

"What's the cargo?"

"Heroin and guns."

A WWII truck waited behind the shop, sputtering clouds of black smoke. The driver in dark green fatigues waved at them to hurry. Zaw stepped on the bumper and held the tarp aside as she climbed in, exhilarated to be outside. But she'd only exchanged one claustrophobic space for another. The smell of machine oil was overwhelming, making it difficult to take a deep breath. Wooden crates wrapped with rope filled the truck's interior except for a tiny, cramped opening near the rear. Zaw explained every vehicle would be stopped and checked for smuggled contraband unless the smugglers paid a hefty bribe. No matter what happened, he admonished her to be quiet, then joined the two soldiers in front. Mallory curled into a tight ball around the ruby.

They left Hsipaw after midnight and traveled along a paved road heading north, deeper into the mountains. After an hour, the truck shuddered to a stop at the first checkpoint. Loud voices shouted as she cowered, sure they would hear the *thump thump* of her heart. Unknown hands opened the tarp, and her closed-shut eyes sensed light from flashlights scanning the crates. She imagined steel hands grabbing her and dragging her from her hiding place. After agonizing seconds, the engine roared to life, exhaust flooding her nose.

The next stop was hours later, deep in Shan army territory. Zaw helped her down from the back. Her stiff joints didn't want to loosen. When she started to ask a question, he put his finger to her lips. Stately teak trees and lush foliage encircled them, but all she could think about was having to pee. Teenagers in tattered uniforms cradled battered Chinese knockoff PKM machine guns as they swarmed the vehicle.

One boy soldier grinned widely. For a brief anxious moment, she thought his teeth were red with blood. Were these people cannibals? But it was only the ubiquitous betel nut. One of their guides shouted at him in a dialect she didn't recognize and the soldier lowered his eyes and turned away. She chided herself for being so foolish. With one guard standing watch, the others set aside their guns and worked silently to empty the truck. Each rope-wrapped crate was burned with the same X-shaped brand. A man in homespun black clothing appeared from the forest, leading a pack of small mules, and the boy soldiers began to load the crates onto the animals.

After a quick visit behind a bat-free tree to relieve herself, Zaw hoisted her on a rustic wooden saddle, straddling one of the mules. The beast was so small her feet grazed the ground. Without a word, they set off in a single file, following two guides up a narrow path. In addition to a machine gun, Zaw carried a handgun attached to his belt. The saddle had no stirrups, so she rocked painfully on the hard saddle atop the bony spine of the complaining creature. She'd never been so uncomfortable in her life.

High in the mountains, they stopped to eat. Mallory fell off the mangy animal, thighs bruised and raw, certain the mule was equally relieved. The rain had stayed away, but the muddy red earth clutched at her shoes. Zaw brought her a leaf-wrapped package tied with jute string and stuffed with sticky rice, sliced chilies, and a pickled egg. As she munched, she stroked the bump of the ruby until she realized what she was doing.

After a short rest, she declined the offer to ride, and the small group set out on foot. The guides spoke softly in a musical language as they smoked cheroots, the fragrance drifting back down the line of animals. A strident bird shrieked a warning.

"What kind of bird is that?" she whispered.

"A vulture." Zaw frowned. "Something large is dead nearby."

Long after sunset, they were finally close to their destination of Mong Pan village. Mallory was more tired than she had ever been. Frustrated by the thick mud grabbing her ankles, she had changed her mind about the mule and ridden on the poor animal's knobby back. Again and again, they had made their way up precarious paths and down into precipitous valleys. Zaw and the others appeared tireless during the long slog. The soldiers admonished them to hurry as day turned to night.

They made their way by the light of the intermittent moon and stars. She felt the difference in humidity on her skin as they trekked lower and entered an area of paddy fields. Lingering smoke from cooking fires and a confused crowing rooster greeted the travelers. When they came to a stop, uniformed men came to lead the mules away. Stupid with fatigue, she was too tired to be afraid, only relieved to be off the animal.

A one-armed, grizzled man saluted Zaw. He welcomed Mallory in Burmese and led them to a nearby wooden house built on high pilings with pigs snuffling below. At the top of the short ladder, she found herself in an expansive, bare room. Two mosquito nets, suspended from beams, fluttered in the far corner like welcoming ghosts. A meal waited on a bamboo mat in the center of the floor.

She yelped in pain from her bruised tailbone as she lowered herself to a cross-legged seat. "Where are we now?"

Zaw's eyes searched the corners of the room. "Let's eat and rest now." His voice dropped. "These people are welcoming but still strangers. We must be cautious." He lifted a bowl covering the food.

"What is it?"

"*Nga htamin.* Turmeric rice with dried fish flakes."

"I'm starving." She snatched a yellow patty with her bare hands and took a bite, ignoring the oil dripping down her chin.

Finishing the spicy food, washed down with a rough and pungent green tea, a young woman arrived to show Mallory where to bathe. After hanging a lamp on a peg, she pointed to clothing on a bench and turned away. Mallory rinsed her underwear first, placing the ruby in her mouth for safekeeping. Pulling on wet panties and tucking the gemstone back into her bra, she wrapped a black cotton longyi around her waist.

Zaw had also washed off the red mud and looked dashing in rust-colored Shan trousers and jacket. The color set off his dark skin tone and brown eyes. His short-cut black hair glistened from the water. An awkward silence fell, relieved by the arrival of the one-armed man. After speaking at length to Zaw, he withdrew down the ladder.

"What did he say?" Mallory whispered.

"I'm afraid tomorrow will be even more difficult." Zaw sounded exhausted.

A dish of candles wavered and flickered in the draft. Throughout the long trek under the chandelier of glittering stars, she'd pondered why Zaw was helping her until a horrible thought crossed her mind. Did he want the ruby for himself? But he could have left her in the forest with no one the wiser. Why was he helping her, and how could she repay him?

"I haven't thanked you," she said. "You are risking so much."

"You're welcome. But the danger isn't over. We are in Shan territory tonight. Tomorrow, we will travel about ten miles and re-enter an area under Burmese army control. Then, we cross the Salween River."

Mallory set the ruby on the mat near the candles, ready to negotiate an agreement. Obligation was expensive, but everyone had a price.

"Put it away!" He recoiled as if the sight of it burned him.

Startled by his response, she sat back. It was as if the stone might burn him. "Why do you hate it?"

"Mallory, this is not something one likes or dislikes. This thing is dangerous for you, me, and anyone who knows of it." He frowned as she slipped it back against her skin. "Are you sure you won't throw it away? There will be less trouble if you are caught."

"Zaw, I know you're jeopardizing everything to help me. But I can't."

"I hope we won't regret your decision." He crawled under one of the mosquito nets. "Now, sleep. Your friend, the mule, will be waiting in the morning."

"I'm not sure he'll be glad to see me."

The candles flickered into inky blackness. Zaw didn't want the ruby. Overwhelmed by fear he might change his mind about helping her, she knew only one other payment method. She'd seen how he looked at her when he thought she didn't notice. On hands and knees, she crept under his mosquito net.

"Zaw?" she whispered.

The quiet was so profound she could almost hear his thrumming heart. She leaned over and touched his chest as if she might soothe its beating. With a groan, he put his hands in her hair and pulled her down.

***

Roosters screaming at the dawn woke her. She crawled out from the netting and discovered a fresh set of clothes. Her mud-covered shoes were clean and like new. The young woman had washed everything during the night and dried it over a fire.

Zaw paced soundlessly before the door, dressed as before in faded green fatigues. "Our transport is waiting." He didn't meet her eyes.

"The same guides and depressed mule as yesterday?" she joked.

Zaw's tense face relaxed for a moment into a smile. "No, they deserted us. You'll be relieved to know we have a new guide. And motorcycles."

"Motorcycles! But I don't know how."

"Don't worry. You'll hold on to me. You'll be more comfortable than on that sorry old mule."

Outside, a long-haired teenager in knockoff Calvin Klein jeans and a Rolling Stones T-shirt stood beside two bright-colored motocross racing bikes. Zaw held out a shiny helmet, and she jammed it on her head.

The village homes were little more than nailed logs, woven bamboo walls, and tin roofs with salvaged metal from WWII. Cho Cho and her grandparent's modest apartment was a palace in comparison. But the mountain air was fresh, and hearty tomato plants filled the small garden in front. The fear and anxiety from the previous days had lifted during the night. After making love, she'd fallen into the best sleep since leaving Rangoon curled around the spoon of Zaw's back. She hoped he would smile again.

The day was brightening; they had to hurry. Engines roaring to life, she hoisted her leg and straddled the bike. She checked the ruby was secure and wrapped her arms around Zaw's waist, laughing aloud when their helmets bumped. They were off, speeding away from the sleepy village through paddy fields and onto a narrow trail leading back into the mountains.

Switchback after switchback, they throttled up one steep hillside and hurtled down the other side, the ever-present red mud spattering up behind their wheels. With the higher elevation, tropical bamboo became teak and pine trees, from jungle to forest within a few hundred feet. The vulture ominously reappeared as if following them.

They passed an old woman trudging along the side of the path, a heavy woven basket balanced on her back piled high with firewood. Bright-colored embroidery covered her black cotton jacket. She raised a hand in greeting, her smile empty of teeth. Each hilltop view revealed yet another hill to conquer, seemingly endless, one after another. Mist pooled and poured between the valleys. Far away, smoke rose from a remote village. And then, finally, a glint of the Salween River shimmered in the distance.

At the midday break, Mallory wobbled off the motorcycle. Though more comfortable than the mule, balancing on the narrow seat was tiring, and her hips and legs ached. Zaw brought over some leaves from a nearby bush. "Sit on these. The red ants are painful if they bite." Though his words were kind, his eyes were empty of the usual compassion.

The guide pulled a canister of Pringles potato chips and a sack of oranges from his bag. Walking over to a pool fed by one of the numerous small waterfalls threading through the mountains, he snatched out a cold six-pack of Tiger beer with a grin.

Zaw introduced their young rock star guide as the son of their benefactor, Khun Sa. The teenager seemed delighted to be sharing a beer with an American and practicing his English. He explained that they would soon reach the car ferry.

"This dangerous place as Tatmadaw have big checkpoint." He spat in disdain at the mention of the Burmese army. "One sit-thu, soldier man, is excellent friend, and make no trouble for us. But always problem. After river crossing, we go Homein town, close kilometers from border."

Mallory inquired where he learned his English, and he told them he attended Singapore University, where he studied engineering. And with that, he stretched out on the muddy ground and closed his eyes for a nap.

The nearby waterfall was much smaller than Anisakan Falls, but the silvery sound of the falling water was the same. She dropped on her back, exhaustion and gravity pinning her to the ground. The vulture circled above her. Rolling into a fetal position, she pressed her cheek into the earth.

A second carrion eater joined the first.

CHAPTER TWENTY-EIGHT

Zaw

Zaw had spent the hours since leaving Maymyo attempting not to notice the way Mallory's oversized fatigues clung to her hips and how her eyes glinted like underwater stones. Weakness grew within him like a jungle vine, strangling his self-control until he had succumbed to temptation and sinned with the foreigner. Her arms around his waist as they followed the narrow paths, her breasts against his back, were all distractions he couldn't afford. He had his own life to consider. His mission to his people. They were getting close to the most dangerous part of the plan. Duty demanded he complete what he had promised, but he regretted his weakness.

They remounted the motorcycles and sped along a trail that soon joined an unpaved road wide enough for a bullock cart or an army jeep. When they reached the checkpoint, they roared to the front of a short line of people waiting to cross. Some wore the traditional clothing of the Akha and Lisu tribal peoples, and others dressed in longyi.

The Salween River rushed before them, filled with tumbling debris from upriver. Zaw cringed that the ferry consisted only of a teak and bamboo raft poled by several barefoot, sinewy men. A Burmese army sergeant, rifle slung over his shoulder, examined people's documents. Another man, sporting the signature reflective sunglasses of Khin Nyunt's military intelligence agents, slouched against a wooden barrier, his bored, unsmiling face turned their way.

Mallory unwrapped her arms from around his waist. Zaw had encountered many dangers in his life as a soldier, but waiting to cross the river that afternoon was the most frightening. In front of them, their guide passed a pack of Marlboro Red cigarettes to the sergeant, grinning and laughing, his words inaudible from Zaw's position, but the fake comradery clear. The MI agent began to amble toward them.

On the bike behind him, Mallory's head and face remained hidden by the helmet, but he noticed her hands glowed white as a signboard. He yanked down her shirt cuffs.

The Burmese sergeant withdrew a cigarette from the pack with agonizing deliberation. Time slowed and stopped, except for the agent's movement, sauntering closer and closer. Zaw went still and sensed Mallory trembling against his back. Everyone had heard of the brothel owner caught smuggling a rare gemstone into Thailand. If Zaw and Mallory were captured with the ruby, the government would execute them.

The soldier at the barricade slid the cigarette pack into his uniform breast pocket.

Zaw tensed, ready to flee. The agent was a few feet away. His head tilted with curiosity.

With a loud laugh, the sergeant waved his hand, releasing them to ride through the barricade. Zaw's motorcycle almost leapt into the air as he charged down the muddy bank and on to the raft. He maneuvered the machine to a stop and stood, gulping breath, balancing the bike between his legs on the heaving raft. His heart pounded like he'd run up a mountainside.

"Oh my God," Mallory breathed in his ear.

"Stay quiet," Zaw shushed. "Don't remove your helmet."

Their guide passed a handful of kyat notes to one of the men navigating the ferry. The man raised his hand to signal no more passengers. With a shout, the men began to pole the raft across the swirling brown river as the setting sun winked behind the tree line.

Zaw thanked God for the luck that had brought them this far, but how long would it last? Soon, he must face a demon.

The crossing was short, and they reached the other side quickly. Zaw gunned the motorcycle up a steep, muddy track to an unpaved road. They were almost to their destination – the remote mountain village of Homein, the stronghold of Khun Sa's rebel Mong Tai Army. Like the Kachin, the insurgent chieftain had fought the Burmese for many years, but his war was a front for other, more illicit activities. Zaw prayed they would be safe and the axiom – the enemy of my enemy is my friend – would hold. Also, he had promised Khun Sa something he desired more than anything: a legitimate voice in the negotiations with the Burmese.

It was dinner time when they arrived. More a town than a village, the financial benefit of the heroin trade was obvious. Homein consisted of a well-maintained road down the center of several dozen solid-looking teakwood houses. Khun Sa's son stopped before a wooden cabin set a little way away from the others. He pulled off his helmet and shook out his hair.

"You stay here. Eat now. Meet father later." With a nod to Mallory, he rode off, the sound of the motorbike receding as he headed back the way he came.

Zaw pushed down the kickstand and helped Mallory dismount. "Take off your helmet inside."

Mallory crawled up the ladder with a small moan and limped into the house. After securing the bike and their bags, Zaw found her inside, collapsed in a heap on the floor. Two narrow beds lined the far wall of the room. A drying towel and singlet shirt hung from a clothesline, and a plastic toy car, wheels missing, was tossed into a corner. He wondered who they had displaced for the night.

"Do we sleep here?" Her eyes searched the room.

"Yes."

A Shan village woman appeared at the door. She knelt and asked, in Burmese, if the guests wanted dinner. She gawked at Mallory as Zaw thanked her and asked where they could wash off the sticky mud.

"We eat soon," Zaw told Mallory. "I assume this is her home."

The young woman reached a finger to touch Mallory's face, and then her hand dropped to Mallory's breast, her eyes bright with amazement.

"What's she doing?" Mallory stepped back, arms crossed across her chest.

Zaw smiled. "She has never seen a European before, except in a movie. Don't be offended. She is asking if you are a real woman or a ghost."

"Tell her to stop touching me."

"Don't worry. She is honored you are a guest in her home." Zaw reached for Mallory's bag. "She will show you where to go. Put on your original clothes. Tomorrow, you cross the border."

The Shan woman brought them rice noodles swimming in a hearty broth, covered with pounded pork mince fried with spicy chilies. Clothed once again in her American jeans and expensive T-shirt, Zaw understood the Shan woman's reaction to Mallory. She was indeed a ghost. A white-skinned alien stepped out from a movie screen. After sleeping with the American and the long trek through the mountains, something had soured within Zaw. Shame, similar to his experience with the execution of the teenagers, ripped at his heart. The spell cast by her beauty was broken. Her tight arms around his waist had become constricting as a python, squeezing the sympathy from his head and heart.

When Zaw had first met Mallory in Rangoon, he thought her an unusual Westerner, sensitive to the customs and culture of the country. But he was wrong. She was just like the others. Another foreign invader looting the resources of his homeland. But he had given his word. Without duty and honor, there was nothing.

"Mallory, we must discuss what you say to Khun Sa."

She glanced up, pretty face suddenly tight with worry. "What *I* say?"

"He will question us about why we need safe passage through his territory." Zaw softened his tone. "I don't know how much English he speaks, so I'll probably do the speaking. You should be prepared. I am uneasy having you meet him in person, but we can't refuse."

At that moment, a soldier arrived, instructing them to follow —the president waited. They followed the young man to a palace-sized wooden villa near the top of the mountainside. With a salute, he left them at the door.

A generator woke, and the entire interior lit up with red and green Christmas lights. A man in jeans and a floral western shirt sat against the far wall on a carved wooden throne. Various swords and horned animal skulls hung above him. Zaw had never met the man, but his reputation for violence was legendary.

"My guests," Khun Sa boomed in English, pointing to low chairs. "Take drink!"

The warlord poured from a liter of Johnny Walker Blue label into chipped crystal tumblers and handed around cigarettes. Host duties accomplished, he sat back on his chair as a pretty teenage Shan girl crept out from the shadowy corner to kneel at his feet.

"Come close," he commanded Mallory. He held up a smudged photocopy of what appeared to be a passport photo. Nodding in approval, he nudged the young girl with his foot, saying something in Shan, which caused her to giggle and blush.

"Why is a Kachin colonel with this American woman, Mallory Jones?" he demanded.

Mallory lifted her head at the sound of her name. Zaw

tried to reassure her with his eyes. But it was bad that Khun Sa knew her identity already. His spy network must be formidable.

"I met her in Rangoon," Zaw said. "As you know, I am working in the capitol on behalf of the National Myanmar Peacekeeping Accord." He hoped to remind the man of their agreement.

"Why were the Westerners in Maymyo?"

Zaw thought fast. Mallory could be very convincing, and it was evident her beauty appealed to the man. Zaw didn't know how much English he spoke, but it might pander to the bandit's vanity if he thought they thought him fluent. All this passed in an instant. He regretted not strategizing their stories, but there'd been no time. Nervous sweat ran down his back.

"Perhaps it is best if the American explains in her own words?" Zaw said, still speaking Burmese. The self-proclaimed Shan president swiveled his lizard head from Zaw to Mallory and back again. He nodded.

One strand of twinkling lights began to pulse on and off. A coded message or a misfiring circuit? Zaw steadied himself, battle-ready. The teen girl frowned and jumped up to tug at the wire until the flashing stopped.

"Mallory," Zaw said. "Please explain why you and your friends visited Maymyo."

She looked at him in wide-eyed alarm. "Everything?"

Zaw didn't know what she would say, but he trusted she would flatter the warlord, which might be enough.

She sat for a moment – eyebrows drawn together in concentration. "I was traveling with two friends from Rangoon," she began. "One of my friends, Geoffrey, heard about a monk – formerly a colleague of Aung San – and thought it would be fantastic to try to meet him. Geoffrey loves history and wanted to hear about the time of independence from someone who had experienced it. He planned to write a book on the subject."

Zaw took a swallow of his drink to cover his amazement at the audacity of her story. He prayed it wouldn't get them both killed, but it was too late to stop her.

"My boyfriend, Thierry, and I thought it would be fun to accompany him and see the north. But somehow, Geoffrey and the monk got into a heated argument inside the hide-out cave where he stayed after Aung San's assassination. I don't know what happened because I was outside, but a huge fight started, and the poor old monk and Geoffrey were both dead. Terrified, Thierry and I jumped into the car without thinking. Then came the car accident, and Thierry fell…" She stopped to take a breath. "I panicked and went back to the hotel. I didn't know who else to call for help. Thank God Zaw came."

A long silence ensued as Khun Sa looked from Mallory to Zaw and back again. His eyes narrowed into unreadable slits. But then something surprising happened. The Shan president and infamous drug kingpin started to wheeze with laughter. He laughed until he wiped away tears. Composing himself, he grabbed Zaw's arm and pulled him so close that Zaw smelt whiskey and garlic.

"You give me what you promised, or you die." He growled in Burmese as he shaped his fingers into a gun and poked Zaw in the chest. He pointed at Mallory and said, "CIA, DEA. All Khun Sa friend."

Still chuckling, he shuffled from the room. His hand rested on the girl's slender neck like a noose. The generator unceremoniously shut off, leaving them in darkness. The earlier soldier reappeared with a flashlight. Only stray dogs with yellow eyes watched them walk in silence through deserted streets.

"What just happened?" Mallory sat on one of the beds. "What did he say to you at the end?"

"He reminded me of my debt." Zaw adjusted the flashlight to illuminate the space between them like a small yellow moon. He felt as if he'd survived a bomb attack only to find he was still clutching a live grenade. "He believes you are a spy, and I think he will try to leverage helping you with the Americans."

"Well, good luck with that."

"Don't underestimate him. He understands more than he revealed. He knows your name and has a copy of your passport picture. I worry your story will unravel. We must move faster. If lucky, tomorrow you leave Burma and enter Thailand."

"What about you? Won't you be with me?"

"Until we meet my contact – a student who fled to Kachin State after the uprising. He now lives in a camp on the border not far from here. Thai authorities keep a close watch but mostly leave them alone. We take the motorbikes as far as we can and then hike to their village. There is a Shan-British woman who brings them money. I pray she will be there and help."

"Hike through the jungle? Is it far?"

"About ten miles. Motorcycles attract too much attention. Both Thai and Burmese intelligence agents monitor the trails. We must be fast but quiet." He didn't mention they would have to hack part of their way through an almost impenetrable jungle populated with dangerous wildlife and buzzing with insects. Many refugees became extremely ill and even died from malaria, dengue, and other mosquito-borne diseases endemic to the area.

"What happens when we meet the former student?"

"Someone will take you by boat to the town of Mae Hong Son. From there, you can take a bus to Chiang Mai, where there is an American consulate. You explain your passport and ticket home were stolen. Play the role of the lost tourist. I hope they will provide you with documents to leave Thailand."

"What about the ruby?"

He groaned. *Drop the cursed rock in the jungle, he thought. Throw it in a river, or give it to one of the thousands of refugees struggling to survive.* For an instant, he saw himself wresting the stone from her. How many rifles would such a jewel buy? He shook his head clear. "You can throw it away."

"You know I can't do that," she said. "I'll never be able to repay you for helping me. If I sell it, I want to share the money with you."

Revulsion crackled through his body. She couldn't see the evil at work. "I don't want anything from that wickedness," he said. "Why did the Buddhist Sayadaw keep it hidden for so many years? What did he fear? One person shouldn't own something so rare. A millennium of want, of *craving*, infuses that rock with unhealthy power. Like you, I feel the pull. But I resist it. As the monk said, it carries a malevolent influence. I want you to take it far away."

"Do you think it made *me* evil?" Her eyes were invisible in the shadows.

"I don't know," he sighed. "But soon, you will *both* no longer be my responsibility. Now, try to sleep. We have another long day tomorrow."

He prayed she would stay on her side of the room. The thought of her white naked body as she'd moved over him made him clamp shut his eyes. There had been women in his life but no lasting relationships. A soldier couldn't make a husband's promise. After a few minutes, he heard her breathing slow. In the blackness, his eyes searched for some bit of light to anchor him. The night filled with the familiar sounds of cicadas, tree frogs, and the first patter of a rain shower.

The path home beckoned in his dreams.

CHAPTER TWENTY-NINE

Mallory

Mallory missed the mule already. Armed with machetes, they hacked east, following a forgotten smuggler's route. The threat of falling and twisting an ankle on the treacherous, slippery hills was constant, but the narrow valley bottoms were the worst. Leaches waited in puddles of rainwater, and poisonous snakes dangled, ready to drop, from trees. Plants with sharp thorns grabbed at them. Malarial mosquitoes swarmed and feasted on their blood.

"Is it much farther?" she asked for the second time within an hour.

"No." Zaw's patient voice had worn thin.

The trail dwindled into nothingness. She doggedly followed Zaw's sweat-drenched back with no alternative, slashing at the chaos of vindictive vegetation. Up went the machete and down. Leaves, thorny branches, tough-skinned vines. *Chop, chop,* like prepping an enormous salad. Ribbons of sweat tracked down her arms, covered in green chlorophyll and sticky sap. The incessant chain saw buzz of insects was driving her crazy. She was hacking at Martin and his rich asshole friends with each *whack, whack* of the blade. *Take that and that, you fucking bastards.* There was no time to worry. Only raise the machete and bring it down. Take another step.

They reached a tree-ringed oasis, and she saw the sky for the first time that morning. Sprawled in mud, she gulped water from a plastic bottle. Zaw slumped to the ground, face camouflaged by dirt. They might be walking in circles. She was lost somewhere in the unmapped mountains of eastern Burma. The green and yellow bruise from Thierry's grip made an aching tattoo around her wrist. The ruby pressed against her breast as if it could fill the emptiness. Stumbling to the edge of the clearing, she vomited until she was empty of everything except loss.

"Are you ill?" Zaw called.

She wiped her mouth and drained the musty bottle of water. How to tell him she'd been sick for a lifetime? A chatter and howl above her head caused her to jump. "What is that?"

"Monkeys. We disturbed their home."

Leaves rained down as something shook the branches. A small face with wicked fangs appeared through the greenery, mouth stretched in anger at the disruption. Another, and then another, arrived, jumping from branch to branch. Zaw threw a rock. The monkey retreated but continued to complain.

"We must move. The noise attracts attention."

They wearily resumed their push through the jungle, accompanied by hornet-sized mosquitoes. Mallory followed Zaw's back as he sliced through the brush, searching for the trail. Both machetes dripped with the forest's green blood. On cue, a crack of thunder shook the earth, and rain started to drench them. Mallory was tempted to strip and let the shower rinse away her wretchedness, but she was already shivering – hopefully not from malaria.

An hour later, Zaw threw down his machete. She almost bumped into his back. An actual trail had appeared, but it was narrow and difficult to navigate without keeping her eyes fixed on the ground. She looked up. A tall, thin man stood in the shadow ahead.

"Colonel!" the man spoke English. "You're late."

"Ko Thant. I'm pleased to see you." Zaw's tight face softened. "Welcome to Thailand, Mallory."

If Ko Thant was surprised to find Zaw Wren with a Western woman, he didn't show it. He led them to his camp, explaining to Mallory how he had come to live in the jungle on the Thai-Burmese border.

"I escaped Rangoon after watching my best friend get shot by a soldier during a peaceful demonstration and thrown into Inya Lake to drown. Soldiers arrested my other friends and took them to prison –or worse."

Just like Cho Cho. Educated, urbane young people forced to remake themselves in a new, brutal reality. She hoped to see her former assistant again but knew it was unlikely.

"I fled north to Kachin State," Ko Thant said, "and stayed near the KIA headquarters with other student refugees for almost two years. That's where I met the colonel." He nodded at Zaw. "Isolated and without hope, we turned in on ourselves. and paranoia forced me to flee again. I formed another camp with a few trusted friends. We dream of returning home to our families under a better government led by the Lady, Aung San Su Kyi." Though he spoke as if discussing a chapter from a history book, his voice trembled. "We've been waiting for five years."

To compare her life and that of Ko Thant was impossible. Mallory belonged to another planet where individuals had the privilege of self-pity. There was no place for such emotions amongst people just trying to stay sane and survive in the mud. The ruby bruising her chest bone reminded her of its potential.

Ko Thant pointed ahead to rough wooden structures scattered along the bank of the Pai River. From a distance, the scene was picturesque – the jade-green stream contrasted with the red of the earth. As they got closer, the homes became simple huts fronted by drooping tomato or pepper plants. A young woman watering her garden was the first to notice them. She turned and ran to the one solid-looking building in the village. Another woman and a man came out and watched their approach guardedly.

"Colonel, we've been waiting since receiving your message," the man said. "Please come in. We are just finishing our lessons for the day."

Inside, about a dozen wide-eyed children sat in a circle on the floor. A Padaung tribal woman with massive brass rings circling her neck and legs sat straight-legged in the corner. Mallory had read about the so-called 'giraffe' women. With a clap of hands, the first woman released the young students from their lessons. Freed from schoolwork, little hands tickled and tugged Mallory's fingers and stroked the skin of her arms. After a few stern words from the teacher, the children filed out, looking back over their shoulders and chattering to their schoolmates. With a stiff but dainty grace, the Padaung woman stood to face Mallory, two young women, each captivated by the other's strange beauty.

"We opened a school for the villagers nearby," the Burmese teacher explained. "We teach them reading and basic mathematics."

The teacher appeared to be a child herself. The first man entered with a three-legged stool for their foreign guest. Another woman arrived with a thermos of hot water and dusty packets of coffee mix. With nods and shared glances, Zaw, Ko Thant, and the third man excused themselves. Mallory's annoyance at being left behind dissipated at the sight of a damp cloth. She wiped the jungle off her face and arms with relief.

The two Burmese women sat like graceful herons, tucking their legs to their sides while Mallory plopped on the low stool with her knees around her ears. "Would you like a tour of our camp after your rest?" the school teacher asked.

"Thank you." What was there to see in such a modest place? "How many people live here?"

"Not including the Padaung village nearby, we are about

twenty," the first woman said. "Though our population fluctuates. We try not to draw attention from the Thai authorities."

Mallory sipped her drink. "Are you all from Rangoon?"

"Most of us, though Ma Htet here," the teacher indicated the first woman, "is from Mandalay."

"It must have been hard to move from the city to live in the wilderness."

"We had no choice," said Ma Htet. Her black eyes never blinked.

Mallory set down her chipped cup. Questions would only emphasize everything they had lost. "How about that tour?"

The evident pride in the women's voices as they strolled through the village and pointed out their achievements was heartbreaking. The tiny refugee outpost had been carved from the forest by unprepared teenagers who had grown up protected by middle-class privilege. Without the donations provided by a British charity organization, they would starve. So little was so very much for them. What would they think if they knew what she had done and why she was in their camp?

She kept touching the itch of the ruby under her shirt. How much rice could it buy? There was no sign of Zaw. The women shrugged their shoulders when she asked about him. The thought crossed her mind that he might hand her to the Thai police now that they were over the border.

"We have prepared lunch for you," Ma Htet said.

In an open-sided structure, another young woman was frying vegetables in a pan over an open fire. Rice simmered in a large pot. As Mallory sat on a bamboo mat, her eyes swept the camp, but Zaw was still missing.

A loud engine suddenly disrupted the simple meal of fried tomatoes and fresh banana shoots. A long, narrow boat trailing black exhaust appeared around the river's bend. All the refugees poured down to the bank, pointing and shouting greetings. Uncertain of what was happening, Mallory relaxed as Zaw strode toward her from the woods.

Ko Thant waded into the shallows at the river to help guide the boat. The boat's captain – a scrawny teen sporting an LA Lakers cap – jumped into the water to steady a woman with long braids piled on her head as she made her way to shore.

"Minglaba!" the woman called to the small crowd as she slipped a satellite phone into the pocket of her shorts. Pleasant-faced, she appeared to be in her mid-thirties. Ko Thant and the others shook her hand, mobbing her like a celebrity.

"That is Millie, the British-Shan princess. She is your transport to Mae Hong Son," Zaw said.

"Where did you go?"

Zaw held up another bulky phone. "I climbed back up the mountain to catch a signal."

Millie approached them with her hand outstretched. "Well, this is a surprise. An American in our camp?" Her accent rivaled the queen of England.

Zaw shook the woman's hand as he introduced Mallory. "This is Jane."

For a moment, Mallory was confused by his use of a different name but understood the benefit of a new identity. How much did the woman know?

"Hello, *Jane*," Millie said. "How do you like our outpost?"

"It's remarkable the students have been able to survive."

"Yes, well, with a little help from friends," Millie's eyes followed the boat-unloading process. "We'll be heading back soon, so say your goodbyes." She glanced at Zaw with raised eyebrows and then walked back to the others.

"Goodbyes?" Mallory had known the moment would come, but it was still a surprise.

"I must return to my work."

"Zaw, how can I thank you?" She put her hand over her chest, confirming the jewel was still there. This was it – the ruby was hers.

Zaw's eyes followed her gesture. "You take it away. That is my thanks."

She stared at his face. Broad bronzed cheekbones, triangular nose, brown eyes filled with flecks of gold, and something she didn't understand until now. Not desire for her, but pity. She shook her head and scuffed her shoe in the dirt. He had rescued her – but from what? She carried a stain wherever she went.

The long-tail boat was ready, emptied of supplies. Millie waved her arm in a hurry-up gesture. Zaw led Mallory to the riverbank and held her hand as she waded out. The teenage captain helped to pull her in. With a yank on the cord, he fired up the two-stroke engine. The boat shot forward like a dragonfly.

The refugees waved from the river's edge, no longer students, but adults clinging to the glory of their past and dreams for the future. Zaw stood a little apart, his hand not in a wave but shading his eyes. Ensuring she was gone. They flew down the bright jade river, skimming the smooth surface. Mallory dipped her hand into the water and drew it out, expecting her fingers to be green. They would reach Mae Hong Son soon and the bus to Chiang Mai.

She began to shout over the engine's roar, but Millie put up her hand in a silencing gesture.

"The less I know about you, the better," she said. "You are nothing but trouble for us all."

"I only wanted to thank you."

Millie barked a laugh. "Thank me? Golly, that's rich from you. "

"What do you mean?"

"Are you really that naive? To think saying thank you adequately covers what these people have risked for you? The Burmese government is always watching, spies everywhere. Those poor students walk a razor's edge; one small slip and they're dragged back to prison for life. And the colonel. What spell did you cast on him to jeopardize his career, his life, for you?" Millie thrust her face into Mallory's and spat, "I hate Americans like you, overflowing with entitlement and the assumption that the world owes you some sort of debt for your Big Macs and MTV culture."

Mallory leaned back, astonished at the woman's vitriol. "You don't know anything about me."

"I don't have to know a thing about you. Just the fact of you here, in my boat, tells me everything."

Mallory kept quiet the remainder of the ride, her thoughts tangled and twisted into a monstrous knot. But she had the ruby, right? She doubted she understood or trusted anything except the comforting feel of the solid stone under her shirt.

The small scenic town of Mae Hong Son rests like an egg, cradled by soft green mountains. Cooking fire smoke hovered over the valley in a gauzy blanket. Wooden chalet-style houses passed by, slower and slower until the teenager shut off the boat's engine, and they glided to a rickety bamboo dock.

Mallory jumped from the dock to the land. She put up her hand in the same stop signal Millie had used earlier. "You think you know who I am." She hefted her bag over her shoulder. "But, actually, I'm much worse."

Mallory didn't take the bus to Chiang Mai and the American consulate. She had someplace else in mind.

CHAPTER THIRTY

Mallory

A massive snake hung from the branch above her head. The jaw of the python slowly opened wide enough to swallow them all – Geoffrey, Thierry, the Sayadaw monk. Mal raised her prized kitchen cleaver to strike, slashing like a crazed butcher over and over until she, too, was dead, drowned in crimson blood.

Mallory woke with a gasp, teeth chattering from the bus's arctic air conditioning, hugging herself for comfort and warmth, the ruby cradled within her arms. What day was it? Was it twenty-two or twenty-five days since she'd first arrived in Rangoon? She'd lost count. Less than ten hours since Zaw Wren stood on the river bank, watching her leave.

The agent had warned that the first bus heading to Bangkok was not direct – it stopped at every town and village. But Mallory bought a ticket anyway and settled into her seat with relief – until the umpteenth stop at a nameless crossroads marked only by the yellow smoke of distant cooking fires. There was nothing to do but think as the bus tires trundled along the narrow highway. She hugged the ruby tighter, pressing it into her breast as if carving a little shelf.

Crumpled travelers snored or stared vacantly at their reflections in the mirror of the window's blackness. The vehicle slowed to a halt, and the driver called out the name of yet another border town. An older woman near the front stood to perch on her toes and pull her bulging bag from the overhead shelf. The door swooshed open. But instead of new passengers, two police officers wearing dark blue uniforms with vivid insignias branded on their shoulders barged onto the bus. The woman fell back into her seat with a bark of alarm. At the back, Mallory froze. She didn't understand what the officials were saying, but the commotion indicated something serious. The unsmiling officers appeared gigantic in the narrow aisle. Each wore a matte-black pistol at his side.

One policeman began to make his way down the center of the aisle, shining a flashlight into each traveler's face. Mallory crouched in her seat. Suddenly, the officer stopped and spoke in gruff Thai to a young woman several rows ahead. The woman rummaged in her bag and handed over what looked like an identity card. Her hand trembled so much she dropped it, and the policeman grunted in frustration as he picked it up. He shone the light on the document and back at her terrified face. With a quick movement, he yanked her to her feet. Her thin arm might snap within his grasp. As she wailed, he dragged her toward the exit.

A petite Western woman rose to block them, shouting in fluent Thai. She put her hand on the policeman's chest –a modern David against Goliath. With a snarl, the other officer spun her around and marched her down the steps. As he did, the first woman melted to the floor, sobbing, and the officer threw her over his shoulder like a sack of garbage. The other passengers looked away as if not to draw attention to themselves.

Mallory peeked at the scene unfolding outside the bus. The two policemen stood at the edge of the road, illuminated by a streetlight swarming with insects, walkie-talkies pressed against their ears. The Western woman, her bright red hair glowing like a beacon, knelt by the side of the weeping woman. The older woman was dragging her heavy bag away from the circle of diffused light.

A man across the aisle clicked his tongue as if dismissing the drama. "Phmah." He lowered his voice. "Many Burmese people come here. Take Thai jobs."

"What did the Western woman say?" Mallory asked. "Why did they take her off the bus, too?"

"She work in camp close to here. Say police have no cause to take woman."

"What will happen to them?"

The man only shrugged and pulled his sweatshirt's hood over his head. Which would be worse for the young refugee – a prison in Thailand or Burma? The sweet women she'd met at the student camp, sobbing and trapped in cages – concrete walls with rusty iron bars. One of the cops might grab her, too, fingers tearing away her shirt, reaching under her bra, snatching the ruby with a snarl. Marching her down the steps, out from the circle of light, into the darkness at the side of the road. Shooting her in the back of the head. As the bus door closed with a hydraulic gasp, Mallory didn't dare to watch.

***

Arrival in gritty urban Bangkok was a shock. Mallory found a tuk-tuk driver at the bus station who claimed to know the location of the Red Rooster Guesthouse hostel. Located in the Patpong red light district on Khao San Road, her trusty *Lonely Planet* guidebook promised cheap and private accommodations. After sixty minutes of a bouncing, harrowing ride through legendary traffic, the driver stopped, pointed at a random building, and told her to get out.

"Five hundred baht."

Ejected onto the sidewalk, she turned in a circle, trying to get her bearings. Thirsty. Hungry. Confounding illegible script street signs. Unimaginable heat emanated from the concrete slow-cooker of a city. Hawkers shouted and cajoled, offering everything from music cassettes to virgins posing before mold-streaked buildings under pulsing neon advertisements. Desperately needing a cold drink, she ventured inside one of the girlie bars. A host with gold teeth waved her through the entrance into a dark room. It took a moment for her eyes to adjust. With a jolt, she realized the six-foot bartender in the tight green dress behind the bar was not a woman but a beautiful man.

"Beer?"

"Just some cold water, please." She dragged her tattered book from her bag. "Do you know where this guesthouse is?"

"You drink first. Watch the show."

Strobe lights flashed to pumping disco music and illuminated a line of firehouse-type poles. About a dozen young women sauntered from the back, each stopping before one of the poles. They wore matching numbered swimsuits and began to mindlessly bump and grind while chewing gum and chatting with their friends over the thumping noise. They could have been folding laundry.

Mallory had once gone to a peepshow on a dare, but that hadn't prepared her to see one of the Thai girls squatting to shoot a ping-pong ball from her vagina into the beer of one of the ogling men. A cheer rose, and the men leaned in as if they might devour her.

The bartender placed a tall glass topped with an orchid before her. "On the house, lady." She wiped the wooden bar free of a sweaty handprint. "Hostel not far. You look for red cock on sign." She tittered. "Not cock, rooster."

After Mallory gulped down the deliciously strong drink, the bartender led her outside to point her in the right direction. In the daylight, the transwoman appeared much older, her makeup peeling behind her ears.

The Red Rooster Guesthouse was what one might expect for four dollars a night – shared toilet down the hall and anonymity. Mallory stretched out on the stained mattress, her room more a windowless cell than a hotel. She pulled a red cord and a small ceiling fan sputtered to life, swiveling as if searching for an intruder. The ruby settled in her fingers like a familiar but unwelcome childhood memory. Each time she held it, she was surprised by its radiance and the mysterious smile hidden within its silky depths. But today, the smile mocked her. The ghosts of her dead friends chittered in the corner as her dead mother gave her a thumbs up. Mal pushed the poisoned rock to the end of the bed, where it rested like a small puddle of blood. Mallory shook her head clear and tucked the ruby back out of sight. There was no chapter in *The Lonely Planet Guide* for murdering jewel thieves. She would have to write her own.

***

The only phone was in the lobby. A full day passed before Mallory finally reached a distraught Cho Cho at the Bagan Inn. The dragon lady desk clerk frowned each time Mallory handed her the number and coins to place the call.

"Where are you, Miss Mallory? We are worried."

How to tell her that the dreaming promises were finished – Mallory was just another in a long line of disillusionments? "I'm sorry, Cho Cho, but I'm not returning to Rangoon."

"What do you mean?" her voice raised an octave.

In a country with few secrets, Mallory didn't want to risk further jeopardizing Cho Cho and her family. The less she knew, the better. "I'm going straight home to Seattle."

Cho Cho began to cry. "They found your friends." Then she started to sob in earnest. "They are dead. What happened?"

Mallory pressed the receiver hard against her ear to drown out the sound of Thierry's head breaking open on a rock, the muffled thud of a falling body.

Cho Cho continued, her voice a sibilant hiss. "There was a Sayadaw, too. The police have launched an investigation."

It was impossible to know if Cho Cho suspected her of

any wrongdoing. But with time, the authorities would connect Mallory to her Burmese friends – if they hadn't already.

"They'll come asking questions. Just tell them everything. You've done nothing wrong." Mallory took a shaking breath. "I'm so sorry…"

The line was still except for soft weeping. But there was one more favor to ask. Mallory lowered her voice to a whisper. "Cho Cho, there's a shop in Scott Market. The owner's name is Daw Khin Myint." She hesitated. Without a broker, there would be no way to sell the stone. "Will you ask her to recommend a gem dealer in Bangkok?"

Cho Cho was quiet for a long moment. Perhaps she'd said too much, revealing her location. Cho Cho probably thought she was crazy, asking about gem dealers after hearing her friends were dead. Mal held back a moan as crimson blood spread behind her eyes and across Geoffrey's elegant jacket – his suit ruined, indeed.

But Cho Cho didn't press for any details. "All right. Call tomorrow. But be safe, boss," she said with a smile Mallory could hear through the phone wire. Cushioned silence remained on the line. Anyone might be listening. She slammed down the receiver. The desk clerk's glare could burn down a house.

That night, the fan in her room developed an annoying squeak that kept her awake, simmering in heat and bitterness. If caught, would the Thai police keep her for themselves or send her back to Burma? Did Thailand have the death penalty, like in the US? The guidebook was silent on the subject of murder, only warning not to get caught doing drugs. Jailtime for possession alone could lock you up for years. *Damn. Damn.* She tossed on her cot of a bed, imagining the worst. *Tick-tock.* Minutes passed like hours.

Near dawn, guilt edged out panic. Maybe she *deserved* to be caught. Prison was for atonement. For learning a lesson. No doubt about her culpability. Or that of her father, sentenced to life for killing her mother. Did he learn his lesson?

Not a chance. She knew the man who had bullied and tortured his wife and child could never change. Violence, along with plasma and red corpuscles, swam in his blood. He didn't deserve to live. Mal shuffled down the corridor, hoping to shower away the sour smell of her guilt, but she knew it was hopeless. She would always be her father's daughter.

***

The overworked air conditioning unit wheezed in the corner of the guest house dining room. An equally overworked waitress sighed. "You wah caw-fe?"

"Yes, please. Do you have a newspaper?"

The woman inclined her head to a table piled up with out-of-date *National Geographic*, tattered *Rolling Stone* magazines, and a copy of that morning's *Bangkok Post*. Mallory lost her appetite scanning the headline *Murder of British Diplomat Tied to Possible Suicide of French Tourist*. The attached article contained little information and lots of speculation. Thankfully, there was no mention of Cho Cho, Zaw Wren, or an American killer.

As she sipped the strong coffee, she peered into a stranger's reflection in the fly-specked mirror behind the counter. The green eyes Thierry had once admired were sunk deep into shadow; her smooth complexion was now coarse with sun and anxiety. Only her long, auburn hair remained the same. Eating could wait. "Is there a beauty salon nearby?"

***

Mallory touched her newly bleached blonde, spiky hair as she trudged up the baking stairwell to the third floor of the guesthouse. No one would recognize her now. Plopping on her bed, she fanned out her remaining money in a kaleidoscope of currencies – dollars, kyats, and baht; counting it twice as if that would make the measly amount greater. She regretted leaving

Martin's envelope of cash back at the hotel; she'd only taken a little spending money for the supposed upcountry weekend trip. Time and cash were running through her fingers like rainwater.

The sound of throbbing helicopters and Wagner's *Flight of the Valkyries* greeted Mallory as she entered the guesthouse's dining room. Half a dozen drunk German tourists seated in the corner sang the operatic accompaniment to the scene in the film *Apocalypse Now,* when the American airborne cavalry rains death from above on an unsuspecting Vietnamese beach.

"Charlie, don't surf!" they chanted as if the movie was interactive.

Mallory ordered the fried rice – uncertain whether her nervous stomach could keep food down. As she debated the cost of a beer, a pretty woman with vivid red hair walked into the dining room. It was the brave woman from the bus.

"May I sit with you?" She spoke with a Northern European accent. "My name is Isabel."

"Sure." Had the woman followed her? Paranoia changed the taste of her food to ash.

Isabel ordered *pad Thai* noodles and a small bottle of Mekong whiskey. The waitress shrugged and slapped away to the kitchen in her oversized flip-flops. One of the Germans tried to smack her ass, but she swatted his hand away with practiced ease.

The Dutch woman followed the proceedings with a grin. "This is a crazy place," she said. "Have you been here long?"

"A couple of days." Mallory looked down at her now cold dinner. "I think I've seen you before."

"Where was that?"

"On the bus from Mae Hong Son to Bangkok. You tried to stop the police as they arrested a Burmese woman."

Isabel shook her head. "Oh, yes, terrible. Were you there? Thai immigration often uses such tactics to prey on weak refugees." She smiled as the waitress set the noodles before her.

"A thousand baht resolved that issue."

"Was she one of the student refugees?"

Isabel looked up with surprise. "Not many Westerners know about them. No, she is ethnically Kayin. They have been fighting the Burmese for decades, but the situation is much worse now. Her family was killed when her village was bombed. She's trying to reach a cousin in the south."

"Why did you help her? It was very brave."

"I belong to a Dutch aid organization based in Mai Sot. We help displaced people along the border." She took a bite of the noodles, chewed, and swallowed. "And I hate bullies."

"Me, too." Mallory smiled at the memory of the tiny woman's palm against the bulky cop's chest. "How long have you been doing that kind of work?"

"Since '89." Isabel's tone turned somber. "They just keep coming."

The waitress deposited a flask-like bottle of Mekong whiskey and two glasses. The rice whiskey went down smoothly, and one flask became two as they ate, cheered the movie, and joined the German tourists in toasting Captain Willard's epic journey up the Mekong River in the hunt for Colonel Kurtz and his final destiny. In the film, the captain successfully navigated into the heart of darkness, accomplished his mission, and lived to tell the tale. The alcohol told her she could, too.

That night, Mallory dreamt of raining ash and the rumble of volcanos.

CHAPTER THIRTY-ONE

Mallory

In desperate need of something to blunt her ferocious hangover, Mallory stumbled to the dining room. The same waitress from the night before slouched in a chair. Her face was tilted up toward a small television set high on the wall, like a flower to the sun. In the daylight, she appeared much younger. Another woman stood in the kitchen doorway, also watching the television. Their expressionless faces swiveled when Mallory entered the room, then returned to their program. The young waitress muttered and sauntered over.

"Good morning." Mallory immediately regretted speaking aloud as the words banged inside her head with little explosions. "Just some coffee and a bottle of water, please."

The server nodded and shuffled away, returning with a cup and a liter of cold water. She cracked a smile. "You like drink Thai whiskey?"

"Never again," Mallory groaned.

"I bring *congee*. Good after much drink."

Mallory doubted she could keep anything down, but she reconsidered when the waitress placed a bowl of steaming rice porridge before her. One bite and the bland food settled her roiling stomach. When the woman came to take the empty dish away, she felt almost cured.

"Do you work all the time?" Mallory asked. "I'm also a cook, but never worked twenty-four hours a day. You're here morning and night."

"We always stay here. I live with sister." She tilted her head toward the cook, who had returned to watch the TV after making Mallory's breakfast. "Home in back."

"Have you been here long?"

"Five year," the waitress shrugged. "Maybe more."

Mallory sat back in surprise. "Where did you live before?"

"We come from Isan village, very poor. Parents sell us to grandmother, come Bangkok."

"Your parents *sold* you?"

The sour-faced desk clerk entered the room. Mallory shrank in her seat. Payment on her room was overdue.

"Granddaughter say you sick, I bring medicine." The old woman hobbled over and placed a blister pack of paracetamol beside Mallory's coffee cup.

"This grandmother Khwan," said the waitress. "She buy us." The receptionist looked different when she smiled.

"Thank you." Mallory popped open the medicine and swallowed a tablet. Maybe she misunderstood what the young woman said. "Are these women your real granddaughters?"

With an arthritic moan, Khwan lowered herself into a chair at the next table. "They good girl. I take for help in restaurant. They bad life in village."

The waitress returned with a bowl of congee for the old lady and dribbled hot sauce over her grandmother's meal. Her sister brought two more bowls. The three slurped and spooned their breakfast in comfortable silence, reaching across one another for condiments and adding more chilies to Khwan's dish without comment.

Breakfast complete, the waitress draped her arm on the back of Khwan's chair in a gesture of familiarity that twinged Mallory's heart. "Grandmother no make us work in girlie bar like other Isan girl. We no make boom boom with farang man."

The tenderness between the little family overruled any judgment she might have on how they had come together. Mallory had also come from extreme poverty to be essentially sold into the for-profit foster care system. At least these women had found companionship, which was more than she had ever known.

"This lady," the cook indicated Mallory, "also cook."

"Where your restaurant?" Khwan asked.

Yes, where *was* her restaurant? "I don't have one." Eyes burning, Mallory leaned her head against the dingy wall. The weizza's promise to remove any curse seemed a long-ago fairy tale.

Khwan's wrinkled face softened. Mallory flinched when the woman took her hand, thinking she might try to read her palm. But the old woman only stroked the back of her hand as if calming a child. "If cook lady need anything, nephew help. He chao pho. Can help. You say me."

The sisters nodded their heads in agreement. Mallory thought the old lady was saying her nephew owned a Vietnamese soup restaurant and had no idea how that might help her, but she appreciated the tenderness.

"Thank you, grandmother. I'll keep him in mind. Now, may I use your telephone one more time to call my friend?"

Khwan's face returned to her usual expression.

Over the phone, Cho Cho gave Mallory the name of a gem merchant, U Tin Tut, in Bangkok. If suspicious about why she needed such a recommendation, she remained quiet. "Please be careful," she whispered.

"Thank you for everything." Mallory took a shuddering breath. "I left some things in my room at the hotel, and since I don't know when I'll be back, keep whatever you want. That includes the envelope in the safe. I want you to have the money as a bonus." After selling the ruby, Mallory wouldn't need Martin's piddling payoff, and the few thousand dollars would be a windfall for the young Burmese woman. The tears in Mallory's voice dried as she added the lie. "It might be a while, but I promise to return to Rangoon one day, and we'll begin a new project."

***

U Tin Htut was a short, balding man who laughed a lot. His office, nestled deep in the Jewelry Trade Center on Silom Road, was small but brightly lit. A heavy safe and a large device that resembled a massive microscope took up most of the space.

"You are a friend of my cousin, Daw Khin Myint, in Rangoon? How may I assist you?"

It wasn't as if Mallory could take out a for-sale ad in the newspaper or set up a sidewalk table next to the bootleg cassette sellers. There was no way of knowing how much the Burmese authorities knew about the ruby or her involvement in the murders. After the scene on the bus, she knew she could be imprisoned just for being in Thailand illegally. The tick-tock of an overwound clock reverberated in her ears. The choking urgency increased by the hour. She was exhausted by nights filled with dreams of natural disasters. There was no other choice.

"I have a rare item that I want to sell. But the sale must be private."

"Of course, all transactions are of the utmost privacy."

"There's some risk."

He shifted in his leather chair. She could almost see his mind working on the pros and cons of dealing with the foreigner. His expression cleared. "Well, my sister did recommend me to handle your business."

Turning away, she pulled the ruby from under her shirt and set it gently on the desk. In the bright light, it looked as if she'd opened a vein. Her innermost secret lay exposed before a stranger – not just the gem, but everything she had done to keep it.

The jeweler's mouth dropped open. He picked it up carefully as if it might explode. He fixed it to the device and peered into the viewfinder. "Where did you get this?"

"I can't tell you."

"This is most remarkable." He adjusted the scope. "I thought it was a spinel, but I am almost certain it is a true ruby. There has not been such a ruby for generations. How is it possible?"

All the stories she'd invented flew out of her mind like dandelion fluff. Does he read the Bangkok Post? This was a terrible mistake. The man would report her. Zaw had been right; she should have thrown it in the river. There was no lie big enough – but it was too late.

"Can you help me or not?"

He stared at the glowing ruby and then back at her, trying to comprehend how she could own such a treasure. The facade of a friendly uncle dropped, revealing a man with a once-in-a-lifetime opportunity before him.

"I am tempted to recommend another broker. Something this valuable is not my usual business." He wiped the perspiration from his upper lip. "But I can't say no to such an extraordinary jewel. Give me a few days to research a price and a potential buyer."

She slipped it back under her frayed bra into the space carved in her heart to keep it safe. She set the guesthouse phone number on the desk. "Please hurry."

***

That week, the hot season arrived in Bangkok like an unwelcome relative from hell. Each scorching breath became a judgment. *Tick-tock.* The sense of time running out became acute – swaths of inflamed, prickly heat covered most of her body. At night she dreamt of falling snow, reaching her hands up to the coolness. But it was not snow. Volcanic ash – hot and burning – singed her hair with a terrible smell. Every morning she told herself she should just leave the ruby with the broker and flee. No looking back. Find a way out of the country. Hop a ship home. An hour later, she laughed at the idea. Scouring the newspaper for mention of the murders and then returning to her prison cell to wait for word from the broker. And wait. Anxiety constantly rippled through her guts, and she dashed down the hall to the squat toilet, voiding her despair into the stinking hole. She would have prayed if she knew how.

In a book from the guesthouse's makeshift library of frayed CIA thrillers and out-of-date guidebooks, Mallory discovered an entire page devoted to the *Chao Pho* –Thailand's infamous organized crime syndicate.

Grandmother Khwan's offer of help hadn't referred to Vietnamese soup but the local mafia.

FINAL CHAPTER

Mallory

On the eighth day of Mallory's stay at the Red Rooster Guesthouse in Bangkok, a black and white missing persons notice issued by the Royal Thai Police appeared on the message board. Though blurry, the image of Mallory was clear enough – the pale complexion, naïve smile, long dark hair. It was the passport photo the Shan warlord Khun Sa had flashed around. Touching her now short, bleached blonde hair, she reminded herself how different she looked – new hair and face, tanned and gaunt from anxiety and nightmares. But still, the clock wound tighter. Khwan, the young waitress, they had seen her before the transformation – would they make the connection? The ruby tittered under her blouse, reminding Mal she needed a new passport and arrival documents if she wanted to leave Thailand.

A scarred wooden reception counter guarded a narrow, always-shut office door at the rear of the guesthouse foyer. Grandmother Khwan's stool sat behind the counter; a Chinese-style mural of a giant rooster sporting vibrant crimson plumage covered the wall behind her. Red Rooster, indeed. The garish hues made Mal's head hurt. A hammer lodged in her brain pounded.

"Sahwa dee kah. Hello." She hoped the sour-faced woman

would remember the tender moment she'd stroked Mallory's hand. And, more importantly, the offer of help from her gangster nephew. Her heart began to bang. "I brought you a small gift in thanks for the pain medication." She held out a plastic bag of the roasted corn she'd seen the woman enjoy.

Khwan snatched it with a grin.

"Grandmother, I have a favor to ask." Mallory leaned against the counter, blocking the view of the notice. Khwan must not make the connection between the missing person poster and Mallory. Thankfully, the notice didn't mention a reward, but the authorities from two countries were searching for her. "I need the help of your nephew."

Mal imagined two thick pythons – one Thai, one Burmese – squeezing the breath from her body as her bones crunched into manageable swallows.

Khwan's jaw bulged as she chewed. "What problem?"

"I don't have a passport."

Khwan swallowed. "Go embassy?"

"I can't. I need to find a *new* passport." Mallory hoped her emphasis on the word conveyed her situation. *Breathe slowly,* she admonished herself. *No panting.*

The woman finished her treat and wiped her hands with a tissue. "Cook lady, big trouble?"

"Yes, big trouble." Without a new identity, Mallory might as well head back into the jungle. Mal realized she was touching the bump of the ruby under her shirt and yanked her burnt fingers away.

"Come tomorrow. Same time," Khwan said.

***

Each agonizing minute seemed like an hour as Mallory gambled that Khwan and her nephew wouldn't report her. That the Burmese jeweler wouldn't sneak up the stairs, break down the flimsy door, and take the ruby for himself. *Tick-tock.* Counting stains on the ceiling, it was easy to imagine prison without parole. Or worse. Her tattered guidebook left no doubt that tourists were to keep away from any dealings with the Chao Pho organization. Like Japan's Yakuza and China's triads, the local group was known to have tentacles in all areas of crime throughout the Thai kingdom.

After midnight, the swiveling fan stuttered to a stop. Mal woke in her sweltering concrete coffin. Mosquitos whined by her ear. The ruby pressed into her chest with comforting pain, murmuring promises of fame and Michelin Star restaurants. Was it a miracle or a curse, as the Sayadaw monk had called it? The weizza from the Shwedagon had promised to remove the curse of her violent, uncaring childhood, but maybe he'd only left room for another. She yelped as she felt something splintering against her skin, drawing blood. Yanking uselessly on the light cord, she held the ruby up to the window's neon orange glow and peered into the heart of the jewel, searching for cracks or fissures. But the only damage she found was her own.

The following day, Mallory pushed open the narrow door behind Khwan's counter. The spacious room within resembled a corporate office anywhere in the world. An attractive man in his thirties sat behind a computer. "You're the American my auntie told me about?" The Thai man spoke English with an Australian accent and looked like a film star with slicked-back hair and a gleaming silk suit. Not at all what she expected. "Sit down," he said.

Conscious of her appearance, she tucked her cheap hundred-baht skirt purchased at the night market under her thighs. "Is Khwan your aunt?"

"Close enough." The man's welcoming tone cooled. "What kind of help do you need?"

Mallory scanned the room, trying to buy some time before coming to the point. Her earlier benign impression changed as she realized the room had no windows. Stacks of rope-bound crates lined the far wall. With a start, she recognized the burned X mark similar to the boxes of heroin she'd seen carted by mules in Shan State. It was easy to imagine horrible things happening in the seemingly innocuous place.

"I need a new passport," she blurted out.

The man's eyes narrowed. "What happened to your old one?"

"I want one that better reflects who I am now." Whatever that means, Mal thought, wishing she'd brought a knife. Her beloved chef knives were long gone. She could have bought one at the same market where she'd bought the cheap skirt. But knives were expensive, and most of Mallory's money was gone.

He steepled his fingers under his chin, causing his jacket sleeves to rise, revealing intricate tattoos on his wrists. He tilted his head as he regarded her, the simple movement somehow terrifying. "I see." He pulled the cuffs, and the tattoos disappeared. "It is expensive."

"I have money. Or I will soon."

His dispassionate face revealed nothing of his thoughts or opinion about why an American woman might need a new identity. His gaze passed over her, calculating her net worth. Could he see the jewel with his x-ray vision? Or was he just another male with the innate authoritative gaze that allowed them to strip any woman naked with a look? As the silence dragged, she became sure he could hear the drum of her heart.

He came to a conclusion. "Ten thousand."

"Baht?" she was relieved.

"US dollars."

Mallory gulped. "Okay."

The man stood, walked to a cabinet, and took out an ominous-looking black case. "Stand against that wall."

"What are you doing?" Her voice sounded frightened even to her own ears. Would he tie her up and call the police?

The man grinned like a shark. "Smile nicely for your new passport picture. Miss...?"

"Oh." As relief washed through her, a name popped into her head. "Stone. Isabel Stone."

Outside the office, in the lobby, several newspapers were spread across a small table. A glaring *Bangkok Post* headline caused her to gasp. As Khwan was busy checking in a new guest, she slipped the newspaper under her arm and raced up the steps. *Death of British Diplomat Tied to Priceless Ruby Theft.*

Though it wasn't a surprise that the Burmese government would connect the killings, it still came as a shock they knew about the ruby. She'd been stupid to think that a country of watchers wouldn't see something and report it to the authorities. She heard the slapping sound of the little boy's feet as he fled from the grotto and saw the iron expression on Joseph's face as she told him she needed a room for another night.

The article was short. The Burmese police had captured the instigators of the brazen jewel heist; they currently waited in Rangoon's Insein Prison for judgment. Mallory groaned aloud as she continued reading. In addition to the dead French tourist and murdered British diplomat, the thieves consisted of a Rangoon-based family and a Kachin army colonel.

Mal threw the ruby against the wall. With a bounce, it fell onto the concrete floor and rolled to a giggling stop. The jewel was intact, but when it hit, Mallory's heart and mind fractured into a hundred broken pieces.

***

The transition from the outdoor furnace of Bangkok to the freezing air conditioning of U Tin Tut's office made Mal's head throb. "Your message said you had news?"

The broker buzzed with excitement. "How does a dealer determine the worth of a legendary, priceless ruby with no provenance?" He addressed her with an oratorical flourish of his hand. Without waiting for a reply, he answered himself. "It is impossible." He wiped his upper lip with a cloth that reminded her of U Hlaing's crisp handkerchief smelling of mothballs. "Burmese rubies of this quality, greater than fifteen carats in weight, are uncommonly rare, and this stone weighs an astounding three hundred ninety-eight carats." He lifted his eyes to the ceiling as if he couldn't believe his own words. "I researched previous auction sales from Sotheby's and Christie's, but nothing was comparable. At the recent gem auction in Rangoon, a thirty-eight-carat ruby sold for $5,860,000, or $153,725 per carat. That would value your gem at over sixty-one million dollars."

Mal choked. "Are you kidding?"

"No." His genial tone shifted from a friendly uncle to a frustrated one. Had he seen the newspaper article? "But even if I can find a customer willing to risk purchasing something obviously stolen, you will only receive a fraction of that value."

"I can't tell you how I got it," Mal repeated for the third or fourth time. The ruby sat between them on a plastic tray, glistening like a tumor ripped from living flesh. She wrapped her arms around the burning cramps in her belly as if to hold herself together. The odor of sulfur filled her nose. Could the man smell it, too? Light ash seemed to drift down from the buzzing fluorescent lights above. Ash from her dream. The same volcanic ash that had carpeted the alley where she'd stabbed her father into bloody jelly.

"All right. We proceed as best we can." U Tin Tut continued, oblivious to the disaster looming in his office. "A market exists for such jewelry. The right buyer must overlook the important issue of provenance to add a legendary artifact to their private collection." he smiled coyly. "Luckily, I have a special customer – an Arab prince – who I think will make an offer. He is flying his private jet to Bangkok, bringing his expert to examine it. I promised him a new-found treasure of the ancients." He squirmed in his chair. "But you must leave the ruby with me while I negotiate a fair price."

It took a moment to process his words. To leave the stone

with someone else. After everything that had happened. The glowing object she had held against her heart allowing it to burrow into her darkest recesses. She'd spent hours, days, with the ruby mocking her, propped up on a pillow at the end of her bed like a tiny tyrant. The ruby she had murdered to keep. The ruby that had ruined the lives of people she'd come to love. Certainty hit her like a truck. The ruby and all it promised wouldn't save her. Money wasn't the answer to what haunted her.

The broker whimpered as Mal grabbed the jewel back and stuffed it into her bra. It burned against her skin down the elevator and out into the toxic heat. The fire-red sky undulated above her head as if she stood under kitchen heat lamps. All the way back to the guesthouse, choking ash continued to fall, the explosion gathering strength, the volcano readying itself to blow.

Two Thai men in suits filled the small reception space. Khwan sat in her usual spot, but her eyes telegraphed trouble. Police. The heads of both men swiveled as Mal stepped into the room. One took a step closer.

"Are you a guest here, Miss?" His English was good.

Mal tried to push past him. Glowing magma flowed through her veins. All she wanted was to be alone and in silence, as the volcano rumbled through her. But the second man put up his arm like a barricade.

"I'm Detective Suwannarat. And this is my colleague, Detective Chaichana. We're looking for a missing American woman." He tapped the flier pinned to the board. "Miss Mallory Jones. Do you happen to know her?"

"What is your name?" The other detective demanded.

She took a fiery breath. "Isabel Stone."

"May we see your passport, please?"

"I don't have it with me," Mal coughed as she swatted at the cinders pouring from her mouth and floating through the air like glowing embers.

The detectives exchanged glances. "It is illegal for a foreigner to be without documentation in the kingdom."

Run. Now. Mal spun around and fled outside to the sidewalk. Escape. A great roar filled her ears – the eruption. The mountain spewing rock from the bowels of the earth. Not noticing her direction, she raced down the heaving sidewalk, a tide of burning lava at her heels.

A taxi honked at her. "Want ride?" the driver shouted.

"No!" she screamed, throat ablaze, coughing, choking with volcanic ash. No more rides. No more false hope from strangers. Her clenched fists cracked open. Her fingers reduced to crispy, charred flesh, scrabbling for the ruby under her shirt.

A sign in the distance beckoned – Chao Praya River sightseeing tours. The river. She ran faster, desperate for relief from the burning pain. Was this what the fifty-seven people who died during the Mount Saint Helen's eruption had felt? Their breath stolen by ash made of glass and minerals from deep in the ground, the hellish place where rubies are born?

But she couldn't reach the water. Too many long-tail boats – just like Millie's – blocked the bank, keeping her from the river's relief. She pivoted – the dock of the tour boat. The weizza cackled in her head like an AM radio host as she tumbled down the plank and onto the deck.

***

The other tourists kept a wide berth from the wild-eyed woman as the sightseeing boat eased into the filthy river, now sparkling and shimmering with reflected lights. They watched her race to the prow and stare down into the churning river. A shrill whistle. Two men in suits shouted from the dock, waving at the pilot to return to shore. One of the tourists screamed as the woman climbed the railing and leaned far over the water as if to jump.

Something glittered in her fist.

ACKNOWLEDGEMENTS

This book is dedicated to my parents, John and Patricia Badgley, who traveled to Rangoon, Burma, in 1957, not knowing how the administrative accident that brought them there would change their young lives forever.

Thank you to Aleksandar Babić, whom I met one fateful evening under a full moon at a Rangoon garden party. And, of course, to Izabel Babić, the best thing we ever did.

According to my Auntie Sein Sein, when my mother went into labor, a Burmese spirit was sitting on a tree branch outside the Rangoon hospital and slipped into my little squalling body as I arrived. Monday born, I was named Cho Lay, or little sweet. As I grew older, my name expanded to include Cho Chin – sweet and sour. I have loved Burmese food ever since.

Burma/Myanmar is in my soul, and I hope this novel will reflect my profound love and respect for that complex, troubled country.

I'm deeply grateful to my steadfast critique partners, Jillian, Carrie, and Melissa, who have been with me for the past two books.

Special mention to my respected Myanmar writer friend and big sister, Ma Thanegi, who checked I wasn't too off-track with some of the details. Any cultural misrepresentations are my own fault.

Thanks to my team at Atmosphere Press, especially editor Asata Radcliff. Hugo House and the Women's Fiction Writers Association have been marvelous resources.

ကျေးဇူးတင်ပါသည် – Thank you

ABOUT THE AUTHOR

LYA BADGLEY writes suspenseful international fiction featuring characters overcoming life-changing odds. She draws deeply from personal experience living in Europe and Southeast Asia. Her life is worthy of a movie – dabbling in the music industry, opening a restaurant in Myanmar, interviewing insurgents for Human Rights Watch, and microfilming documents for the Tuol Sleng Museum of Genocide in Cambodia. A dedicated environmentalist, she has served as an elected city councilmember and activist. Her first novel, *The Foreigner's Confession*, set in Cambodia, was released in February of 2022. She currently lives in Snohomish, Washington, and is busy writing her third novel.

If you would like to stay updated on Lya's writing, follow lyabadgleyauthor on Facebook and Instagram or sign up for her newsletter on her website – lyabadgley.com.

Please check out Lya Badgley's first novel,
The Foreigner's Confession.

An unexpected, mysterious discovery in Cambodia leads
Emily Mclean on a journey through the country's painful
history and toward personal redemption.

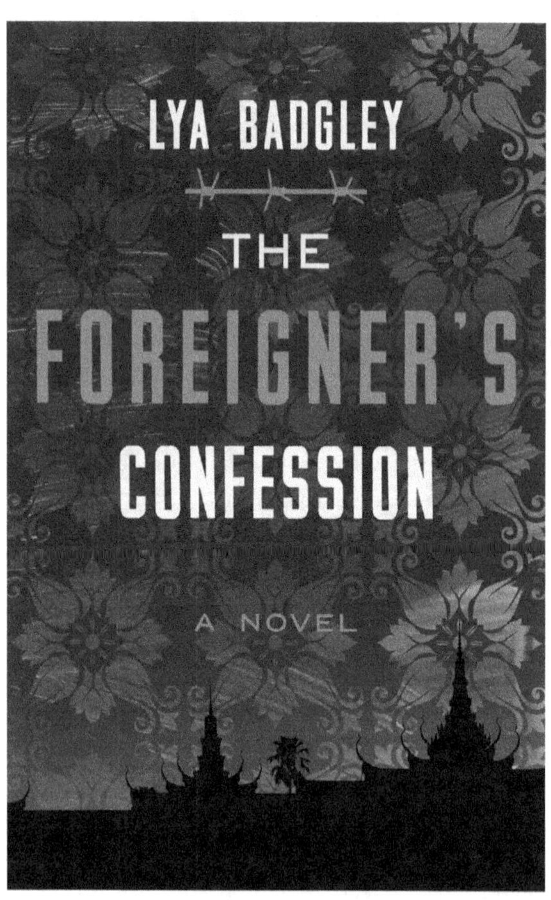

9 798891 320581